When the Caged Bird Flies

Louise Shelley

Published by Clink Street Publishing 2021

Copyright © 2021

First edition.

ISBN:
978-1-914498-31-2 - paperback
978-1-914498-32-9 - ebook

It's not just our differences that divide us.
It's our judgement about each other that does.

Margaret J Wheatley

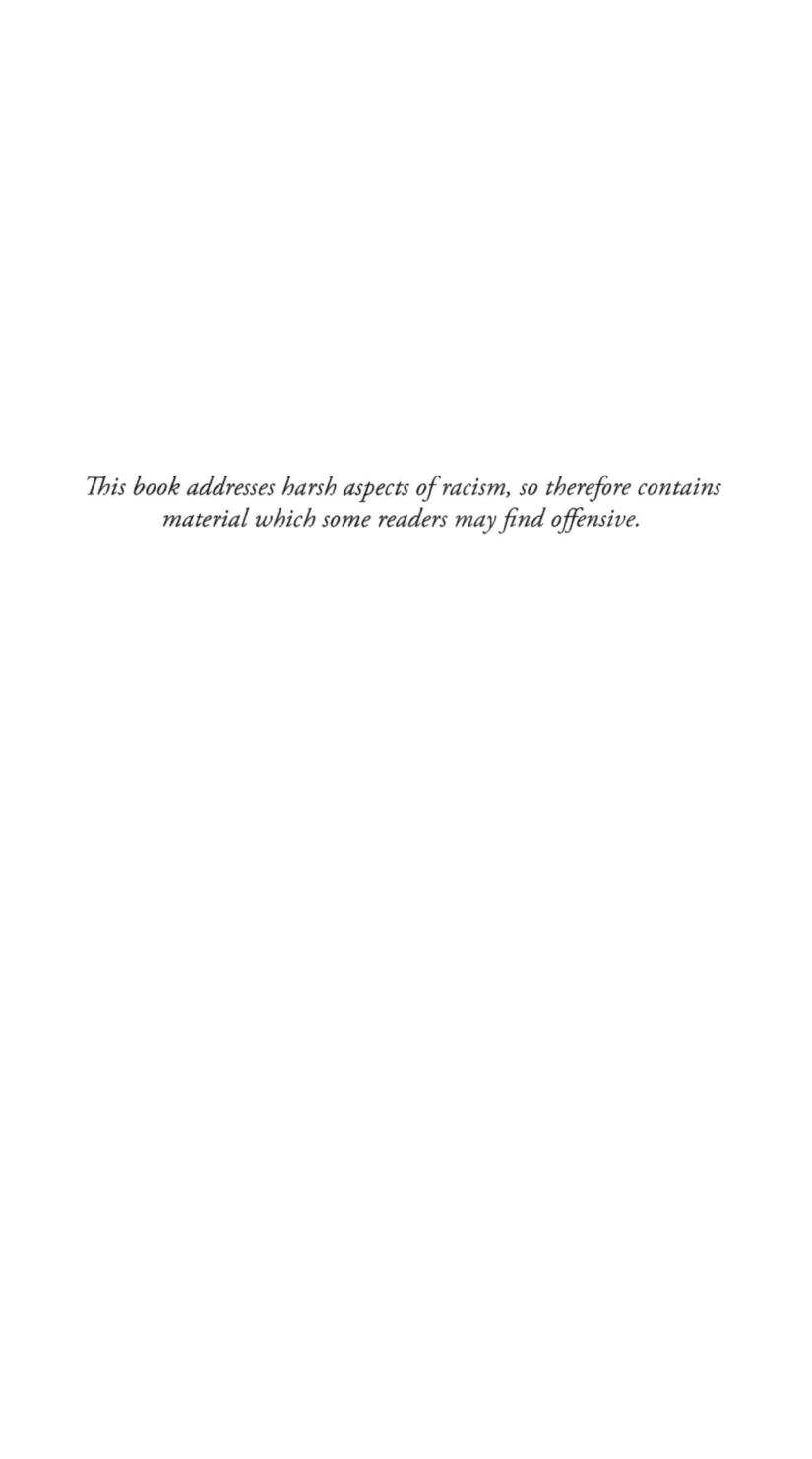

This book addresses harsh aspects of racism, so therefore contains material which some readers may find offensive.

Prologue

'Drink up lads. It's time.'

'Aw come on Trevo, it's not often us lads get to meet up. We've still got a lot of reminiscing to do.'

'Well go and raid your drinks cabinet at 'ome then. You can reminisce all you like in your own 'ouse.'

'The Welcome lets its customers stay until two in the morning behind locked doors.'

'In that case, shove off down the Welcome. I don't go in for those tricks yere. This is a decent drinking establishment. Not like that spit and sawdust shed. The Welcome! Huh,' Trevor scoffed, 'more like the Unwelcome Inn.'

'He'll be expecting his customers to wear a suit and tie next, and having a concierge at the door.'

'CONCIERGE,' Trevor exclaimed indignantly. 'What the hell's that, when it's at 'ome?'

'Posh bouncer to you.'

'Well speak English to me then. Not any of your fancy university talk.'

'We don't speak Sidwegall. Darren speaks Aedre, you may understand that. Baa, Baa, Baa.'

'On that note, I best get going,' Darren stood up, grateful for the interruption.

'Aw hang on a bit,' said Graham, 'you've only had one pint all night.'

'Gotta go over the Sceard haven't I, and can't drink any more, as I'm driving.'

'That's your fault for living in Aedre,' at which Sean and Gary guffawed.

'I'd better make a move as well,' said Gary. 'Marie will be wondering what I'm up to, if I stroll in way past closing time.'

'What happened to us all?' Graham raised his shoulders, palms flat to the ceiling.

'Marriages and mortgages, that's what,' Sean answered.

'How is your Marie these days?' Graham enquired.

'Better now she's part time, to look after the toddler. Banks ain't what they used to be. They used to be good places to work. Now they want their pound of flesh, like everywhere else. It's all target driven these days. We're lucky, we still get a discounted mortgage. They've stopped all that now. She still reckons she works full time though, with all the housework, and looking after Ben. I said you were doing housework when you were working full time. "All right for you," she says, "you don't see half of what I do." What does she think I do all day then? Its hard graft being an engineer.'

'My missus is the same,' Sean commiserated. 'Thinks it's cushy working in an office. As if I'm sat back in a comfy chair. I'm bent double all day, pouring over a sea of figures. Then I've got the boss on the blower. Wanting to know when he can expect the end of the month report. Trudy thinks it's the computer that does everything! Computers haven't made my life any easier; I can tell you. The things break down, which gives my staff an excuse not to work. The other morning, Sandra was there painting her nails. What can I do?' he said resignedly.

'You can say, "That should be Tippex in your hand, not nail varnish,"' said Graham. 'Computers,' he continued sardonically, 'my lad is never off the thing. I had to get him from his bedroom the other week. Come on I said, your mother has called twice to say your dinner is on the table. "I'm playing Battle of Midway," he says. "You'll be having a battle with your mother, I said, if you don't get down them stairs in the next three minutes."'

'I'm not telling you gentlemen again,' Trevor's voice boomed. 'If you're not out that door in the next five minutes, I will physically throw you out.'

'Ok, ok, we're leaving,' Graham held his hands up in submission, while they gathered their jackets, and made their way towards the door.

They stood together outside the pub, under the stark lights which illuminated the white painted walls. They discussed when they would next meet. A discussion which lasted about fifteen minutes, before they said their goodbyes.

'Watch out for the White Lady,' Graham shouted to Darren who was making his way to his car.

'If I see her, I'll give her a lift,' Darren shouted back, as he opened his car door.

Darren was glad of the drive home, which would take him over an hour, but it would give him a chance to come down from the buzz of an entertaining evening. An evening spent with friends he had met during university, and had not seen for some time. He pulled out of the car park, and followed the road out of the village. There were houses either side of the road. They were not emitting any electric light through the windows. He felt he had the road to himself, as the streets were at their quietest, this late hour of the night. The houses became more sparsely distributed the further he got from the village, where the surroundings turned into fields and trees. A certain percentage of the house free land was visible due to street lamps flooding light from above. He knew though, what lay beyond that which was out of his visibility range.

He cruised along enjoying the peace and solitude. The only audible sound being the drone of the engine. The aroma of lime seeped out of the air freshener hanging from the car mirror just above him. He became lost in thoughts of the evening just spent, as he turned on to the mountain road of the Sceard. The road ascended slightly, but would gradually become steeper and steeper, as it coiled around the mountain. He noted with satisfaction the night was clear, but he was still eager to move past the mountain peak, before the mist spilled over the mountains, and rolled down into Aedre, where he lived. The gradient was now becoming more elevated, so he slipped the gear into second, ready for the climb. There were no streetlights to guide him now, only the moon, stars, car headlights and cat's eyes which lined the middle of the road. Cat's eyes. What a marvellous invention he thought. Made night time driving so much easier, and probably saved a lot of lives on roads such as this. He was aware of the practically vertical slope on his left. An advantage to driving at this time of night he reasoned, was no other traffic. The road was not wide enough to easily accommodate another vehicle travelling in the opposite direction, although it was probably as wide as any other non-major road, but the sheer drop on one side meant there was little room for manoeuvre. There were also some sharp turns as the road wound around the mountain. This was where cat's eyes came in handy, as they gave warning of any directional changes. Ah, cat's eyes, he returned to his previous line of thought. A gift to night drivers. Yet, the person who invented them had died penniless apparently. Imagine a world without cat's eyes, he mused. The inventor should have made millions.

There was a sharp drop in temperature now, so Darren switched on the air system to blow out some warm air. He turned a corner, and exhaled a deep sigh on seeing the warm, orange glow of a part of Aedre down below. He sat back in his seat, and loosened his grip on the steering wheel, as he felt the descent of the road beneath him. He moved the gear into third, with his foot hovering over the brake for the sail into Aedre.

The decline became more and more gentle. A smile came over his face, whilst he mentally replayed the evening's events. That Graham is a card he ruminated. The things we got up to in uni. It was Graham who had persuaded us to join the rowing team. 'Come on lads, we've got to do something. We can't spend all our time drinking and watching tele.' 'No, we'll work sometimes,' was Gary's response. Graham was the biggest drinker amongst us, Darren lightly chuckled. That weekend we went away with the rowing club. There was only one pub in a ten-mile radius. We'd had a right skinful, and then couldn't remember where the campsite was. We were staggering around, no one about to ask.

We came across a cottage. No light on, and Graham had the bright idea to knock on the door and ask for directions. 'It must be gone midnight,' Sean slurred, 'they'll call the police.'

The road now levelled, he had a straight run, so he picked up some speed. He was enjoying this reverie, when in a split second a figure emerged from the blackness. Right in front of him. Darren's body went rigid as the car came to a sudden halt. He had slammed on the brakes, and his arms were straight out in front of him, fingers clasped tightly around the steering wheel. His mouth had fallen open, and his eyes were bulging from his head. Time seemed to be suspended in that moment, when the car door opened, and a female bolted into the passenger seat. 'DRIVE ON,' she practically screamed, face fixed straight ahead, body tense and stiff, eyes wide with terror.

Darren's senses seemed to go into automatic mode, as he pushed the car into first gear, and eased his foot off the clutch, so the car slid forward. As soon as he had turned off the Sceard, Darren slowed down to a stop at the side of the road. This stretch of road was still isolated, despite not being a part of the mountain road.

'DON'T STOP, DON'T STOP,' the girl beside him shrieked hysterically, looking frantically behind.

'It's OK, It's OK. You're safe now,' Darren spoke calmly and put an arm around the girl's shoulders. His attempt to comfort her was to no avail however. He therefore decided to continue driving slowly. He reasoned he should get the girl talking, as maybe this would calm her down.

He looked over to her, and guessed she was in her early twenties. Brown wavy shoulder-length hair, a lot of makeup, powder caked into her cheeks, and she was dressed all in WHITE! White jacket, white blouse and white trousers. This was odd he thought, even though the style of clothing was very fashionable at that time. People normally have some splash of colour. He could see her clothes were heavily bloodstained.

'Have you been in an accident?' Darren glanced at her. His leg muscles had relaxed a little, and his breathing had returned almost to normal.

'Yes,' she said breathily. Nodding her head slightly, but keeping her gaze straight ahead. Her voice had decreased considerably, and her movements were not so jerky.

'Were you driving?'

'No.'

'Are there others there?' Darren's voice was raised with alarm, as he slammed on the brakes.

'WHAT ARE YOU DOING. DON'T STOP,' she screamed again, and started to spin around, looking wildly out of the back window.

'OK, OK, it's fine, just calm down.'

'JUST DRIVE.'

'They may be injured; we should go back and check.'

'There was only one, and I saw 'im walking away,' she said through a shaking voice

'He's probably gone to get help.'

'Maybe,' she mumbled.

'Okay, here we go. There's no danger now. Everything is going to be just fine,' Darren said with as much assurance as he could muster.

'What's your name?' Darren glanced sideways towards her.

'Amanda'

'I'm Darren. Nice to meet you. Where do you live, Amanda?'

Chapter 1

'Ow's your mother enjoying her new 'ome,' the manicurist asked, whilst painting the nails of a woman in her fifties, with a rich plum-coloured varnish.

'Oh, much better, since she moved to the bungalow. Well, they 'ad to move her, she couldn't cope with the stairs.'

'Is she missing the neighbours? She lived in Markham Street for years, didn't she?'

'Oh aye, since she got married, so that would be fifty-five years. She found it strange at first, but there's a school nearby, and the children wave to her every morning on their way to school.'

'Aw well, that's nice, and she'll soon get to know the other neighbours.'

'Well, there's a few elderly ones living around there. She was chatting away to a lady over the garden fence when I was there last Sunday. Talking about the war, and when the Yanks were in the villages.'

'Aw, it's good she 'as someone to talk to.'

'What are you up to this weekend then?'

'Neil is bringing one of his work mates 'ome to tea tonight. A bloke from Casteldaeg. So, something different.'

'You never know. Maybe a handsome young man for you.'

'Oh I wish. Well that's you done Mrs Wilkins. You're all ready for the weekend now.'

'Aw thanks Amanda, and you 'ave a nice weekend as well love.'

'Well I'll be yere again tomorrow, and Saturday. See you in about three weeks if I don't bump into you before then.'

Amanda started to pack away the bottles of brightly coloured varnish from her worktable. She was able to reach the second shelf, if she stretched her calves, as at five feet two inches, she found it difficult to extend her arm that far. She had to use the steps if she needed anything on the third shelf. Her hair was a chestnut brown colour, thick and wavy, as she had a semi-permanent wave put in by her hairdresser, as well as a few golden blonde tints. She wore a lot of makeup. Thick heavy foundation, which made her look as if she had a permanent suntan. Mascara and rich, but never garish, shades of lipstick, deep pink, brown or red. She rarely left the house without makeup, and many times she would put on makeup, even if just staying in the house. She was of a bubbly nature, which meant she was well suited to being a manicurist. A role requiring much social interaction. To her clients, she was as refreshing as a sparkling soda.

'That's me done then,' Amanda said whilst adjusting her hair in the mirror. 'Night Abigail, night Jessica, see you in the morning.'

'Yeah, goodnight, look forward to 'earing about city boy tomorrow.'

There was a slight bounce to Amanda's step as she made her way home. She was on the plump side. Cuddly, her friends and family called her. 'You don't want a skinny one, do you?' her brother Neil would say. Amanda lived with her parents and two brothers. Neil the younger, and shorter at five feet nine inches. He had a roundish face, with a few freckles, and dark auburn hair. People referred to him as a cheeky chappie. At twenty-three, he was four years older than she. Her brother Wayne at twenty-five was the more serious one. He had dark brown hair, and thin wire-rimmed glasses. He was an electrician with the fire service, and was very active within the union. Neil worked at Fordmans, a local factory, which made parts for machinery.

'Yere's our princess,' Neil's voice greeted Amanda as she walked through the door. 'Come in yere and meet Desmond.'

'Hello, I'm pleased to meet you. I've heard so much about you,' came a low resonant voice. A black hand extended towards her. She breathed in sharply, and got a whiff of cologne, as she timidly put her hand in his.

'Hello,' she replied, looking up at him. Her voice, whilst not high-pitched, had a shrill to it. Now however, it sounded anaemic. She had never seen anyone with eyes as deep and brown as this man's. He was over six feet tall. His hair was of tight black curls, close around his head. Some of the strands were shining in the light. He had a well-trimmed beard, and full lips, through which he gave a wide smile. His perfect white teeth, were like milky pearls.

'I'll just go and get changed,' Amanda murmured.

'Leaving so soon?' Neil grinned mischievously.

'Oh you know I 'ave to get changed as soon as I come 'ome from work,' her voice was quieter than normal.

'You're not always in such a hurry. Sometimes you sit down for ten minutes.'

'You don't have to get changed at all,' came Desmond's deep-toned voice. 'You look amazing.'

'Oh, get on with you,' she managed to mumble.

'Not at all,' returned Desmond through his broad smile.

'Oh 'ello Samson,' Amanda gently stroked a ginger cat, curled on an armchair, in a puddle of sunshine, who mewed indignantly.

'Aven't you forgotten something?' Neil was pointing towards her handbag, with a big grin, enjoying her discomfort, as she was making her way to the stairs.

'Oh yeah,' she said in a tiny voice, and quickly grabbed her bag and walked to the stairs as quickly as she thought appropriate.

The house smelt of radiated heat. When she returned tentatively from upstairs, everyone was seated at the dining table, which practically filled the room, along with the welsh dresser, which took up approximately three quarters of one wall. The window which looked out onto the small front garden and street, let light flood in through the net curtain, even though the houses opposite could be seen. The table was laid with the little used china. There was ham from the local delicatessen, salad, and cake from a box. Amanda gingerly took her seat, trying to avoid the temptation of staring at Desmond, as she felt if she did, she would not be able to take her eyes from him. She kept her gaze low to the table, but was able to see his chest, and the chiselled muscles over which his shirt stretched, buttons straining to keep it together whenever he straightened his shoulders. The conversation was light and the clink of cutlery against china could be heard during pauses.

'I 'ope you don't mind me asking Desmond,' came her mother Mair's voice, 'but where do you come from?'

'No, I don't mind you asking at all Mrs Williams. I'm from Casteldaeg.'

'Yes,' Mair said slowly and cautiously, 'but where are you really from?'

'I was born in Casteldaeg.'

'Yes, but where are you from originally?'

'What my mother is too shy to ask, Desmond,' Neil spoke with amusement, 'is which part of Africa are you descended from?'

'NEIL! Don't be so rude,' there was a look of horror on Mair's face.

'That's ok,' Desmond laughed, 'My parents are from Jamaica. Their descendants were dragged from Africa to work as slaves on the plantations.'

'That's awful,' Amanda tried to sound indignant, but her voice was still weak.

'They were the lucky ones,' Desmond continued, 'They survived the journey. My parents came over to England in the fifties, when the British government was looking for workers.'

'Do they ever think of going back?' asked Amanda's father Gerald.

'Back to Jamaica or Africa?' Desmond fixed an inquisitive look on Gerald.

'Well.' Gerald fumbled over his words, 'I would have thought it may be better for them to be with their own kind.'

'Their country would be the one they were born in,' Wayne jumped in. 'There was a resettlement programme in America, where the African-Americans were returned to their native Africa. It did not work of course. It was a different culture for goodness' sake. The people had lived under Westernisation for all of their lives. I've never heard of such a stupid idea.'

'This food is delicious Mrs Williams,' Desmond enthused. 'You sure know how to put on a first-rate spread.'

'Oh it's nothing really,' Mair glowed with pleasure.

'Nothing! You'd be hard pushed to put on a meal better than this. It would cost a fortune in a restaurant.'

Desmond asked Mair if she was born in Aedre, and what it was like growing up in such a beautiful place. In between her reply, she kept urging him to help himself to more food.

'Right, well you lot go into the sitting room. Whilst I wash the dishes.' Mair stood up, when everyone had finished eating, and started collecting plates.

'I'll 'elp you Mam,' Amanda quickly grabbed some plates.

'Ooow, you're eager today. You're normally not so keen,' Mair replied.

Amanda could hear a television voice in the distance, whilst she dried the dishes. The voice was telling the viewer the benefits of using a certain type of moisturiser.

'Knock that thing off,' she heard Gerald say, 'Bloody rubbish. I'll watch the news later.'

Amanda left her mother to wipe the remainder of the dishes, and joined the men grouped in the sitting room, drinking lager and ale from glasses. The smell of cooking lingered, although not as strong as the aroma from the kitchen. The walls of the sitting room were covered in pastel-flowered wallpaper. There was a picture of a Parisian scene hanging on one wall, a replica of an oil painting. Desmond thought the sitting room presented a life of its own. There were photographs of babies and children, at various stages of their lives, on a sideboard, alongside the entrance door. Next to trinkets from various seaside resorts. There was a wedding photograph on the mantelpiece, but Desmond's gaze was mostly drawn to a childlike drawing, in garish primary colours on the windowsill, of matchstick humans, boxes and circles representing houses and trees. The picture was signed in crayon, by Amanda aged five.

Gerald was sitting in a sagging beige armchair in the corner, from which he'd dismissed the cat. Neil and Desmond were on one of the two-seater sofas. Wayne was on the other sofa, so Amanda sat next to him. She did not know where to settle her gaze now the television was not on. She picked up the newspaper, which she normally flicked through. Today, she spent more time on each page.

'Remember the day the pit closed?' she heard Neil say. 'We went on a right bender. Old Pikey told his missus she wouldn't be seeing 'im for three days. The local pubs arranged a collection, and laid on free booze and a buffet.' Neil raised his hand to his mouth, in mimicry of taking a drink.

'I were proud to be a miner,' Gerald's chin and shoulders rose slightly. 'We were part of history. They took that away from us.'

'Aye, it was a ready-made life,' Wayne replied with sarcasm. 'There was nothing else around, and it was exploited. Conditions, pay, there was no competition. Those who did protest were blacklisted as troublemakers. Names passed to other mine owners.'

'Yere he goes with his Union talk again,' Neil raised his eyes towards the ceiling.

Gerald belonged to that generation of men, for whom the rules of gender were sharply differentiated. That dying breed where women were not expected to pursue a career after marriage. Being a housewife was considered a full-time role. Coal elements had transmuted into his skin, giving him a grey pallor, like the skin of many miners, who had taken on the colour of their surroundings. He had thick, dark, out of control eyebrows. His hair, although mostly grey, contained more black than Mair's. He was made redundant in his early fifties, when the mines closed, and he had not been able to get another job. He couldn't imagine doing anything other than mining however, and neither could anyone else, who knew him well. He was lucky, in that he was not one of the ones to have had his body etched and gouged by mining machinery. His father had also been a miner, as had Mair's. Gerald's father had gasped the last years of his life away.

Amanda had moved back to the kitchen, as soon as Mair joined the others. She pretended to be preoccupied with putting away dishes and plates. Her heart quickened when she became aware of Desmond watching her from the doorway. He was the height of the doorframe.

'Neil tells me you work as a manicurist.'

'Yeah, that's right,' her voice although not as weak as previously, was quieter than her normal pitch.

'That's a good job.'

'Not really. I trained as a beautician, but it was the only job I could get.'

'Not at all. Making women feel good about themselves. It's a great job. Bringing a bit of joy to their lives.'

'We 'ave a laugh as well,' Amanda picked up a little, overcoming some of her shyness. 'They give me all the goss. Tell me what's going on in the villages. Tell me all their problems too, unfortunately.'

'So, you're a bit of counsellor as well then?' Desmond laughed. 'I bet they didn't teach you that at Beauty College. I don't think you realise just how skilled you actually are.' Desmond moved closer towards her.

'Ow long 'ave you worked at Fordmans?' Amanda averted her gaze back to the plate she was putting into the cupboard.

'Three years. And you know what. This is the first time anyone has invited me to their home. I've been to the pub with the guys many a time, but never to their houses.

'I expect it is quite dull yere compared to Casteldaeg.'

'Not at all. It's beautiful. The mountains. I would love to walk up the mountains, but when I ask one of the guys to walk up with me, they just look at me as if I'm mad. "What on earth do you want to walk up there for?" they say, "there's nothing up there!"'

'I'll walk up a mountain with you,' Amanda said then took in a sharp breath, as if trying to recapture the words she had just spoken.

'Would you?' Desmond's face lit up.

'I've come to see what you two are up to,' Neil appeared at the door.

'I was telling Amanda how much I'd like to walk up one of your mountains, and she kindly agreed to walk up with me.'

'Did she?' Neil said with a knowing smile.

'It's very steep,' Amanda came over all shy again.

'He can cope with it,' Neil said with mock derision. 'All this jungle blood,' he squeezed Desmond's bicep between his thumb and forefinger.

'Watch it,' Desmond grinned. 'Right then, that's all settled then.' He turned back to Amanda. 'How about a week Saturday?'

'I'm working then. I get one Saturday in three off, so it will 'ave to be the Saturday after.'

'Two weeks Saturday it will be then,' Desmond said with finality.

Chapter 2

The Saturday morning had finally arrived. Amanda had been unable to think about anything else since Desmond had left the house that Thursday evening. She spent the rest of the evening and the following evenings, floating around the house, unable to settle. She had risen early, in a dilemma over what to wear. She was relieved to see it was not only a dry day, but as an added bonus, the sun was shining. After rifling through her wardrobe, a number of times, she opted for shiny tracksuit bottoms, a jumper and trainers. The house was filled with the aroma of lemon-scented polish. Saturday morning was the time her mother spent having a thorough house clean. Mair, despite not having yet reached her mid-fifties, looked about eight years older. She always seemed to be wearing a dark blue overall, which made her appear dowdy. Such overalls were fashionable amongst many women in the villages. Mostly those in their late fifties. Mair, in fact was one of those women, whom one imagined had looked that way all their lives.

Amanda looked at the toast on the plate before her, with a crescent moon shaped bite taken out of it. She had eaten little, and was constantly looking at the clock. The seconds seemed to ache by. He said he'd be here at nine she thought. It's five to nine now. She hovered around the passageway, the muscles of her stomach tightening. She could hear Mair, as she moved around the house with purpose. When the knock on the door came after a ten-minute wait, she resisted the temptation to open immediately. When she did, Desmond was standing there, with his wide smile, dressed in jeans, sweatshirt, and a light sports jacket, holding two bunches of yellow roses.

'I hope you've got your walking boots on,' he said through his smile.

'Come in,' Amanda took one of the bunches of roses he offered.

'Lovely flowers for two lovely ladies,' he grinned, handing the other to Mair, who appeared from the kitchen.

'Oooh, they're beautiful,' Mair cried out, 'but you shouldn't 'ave.'

'See it as a token of thanks for that lovely meal you gave me.'

'Not at all,' Mair could not take her eyes from the roses. 'It was a pleasure.'

'The pleasure was indeed mine,' he grinned.

'They're lovely. I'll put them in some water,' Amanda took the bunch from her mother, and disappeared into the kitchen.

'Are you ready to go out now, or would you rather sit down first?' she enquired on reappearing.

'Go out?!' Mair said with astonishment. 'You 'aven't 'ad anything to eat. Sit there, and I'll make you both some bacon and eggs.'

'Nothing for me, thank you Mrs Williams, as I had a hearty breakfast before I came out,' Desmond patted his abdomen.

'Oh, call me Mair.'

'Alligator meat was it?' Neil emerged yawning from upstairs, dressed in pyjamas, hair dishevelled. He grabbed the newspaper and threw himself into an armchair, where he splayed himself, and opened the paper.

'NEIL!' Mair cried out. 'Don't be so rude. Take no notice of 'im Desmond.'

'Don't worry,' Desmond laughed, 'I'm used to him. It was impala meat actually.'

'He probably doesn't know what an impala is,' Amanda scoffed.

'Do you?' Neil looked at her with raised eyebrows. 'Come on 'en clever clogs, what is it?'

'Kind of animal innit.'

Neil harrumphed, and went back to his paper.

'Neil thinks it's a car,' Desmond grinned.

'Oh why don't you go back to bed, you useless lump,' Mair said to Neil, but without any malice.

'Nothing for me either Mam,' said Amanda

'You've 'ardly eaten anything this morning.'

'I'm just not 'ungry.'

'You can make something for me then Mam,' Neil said without looking up from the newspaper.

'I'll give you breakfast. You'll have a clip around the ear, if you don't shut up.'

'You're asking the impossible now Mair,' Desmond said through his grin.

'I don't know 'ow I put up with it,' Mair said shaking her head.

'I have to, eight till four, five days a week,' Desmond quipped.

'We'll get lunch at the Comfort Café,' Amanda said.

'No you won't,' Mair retorted slightly admonishingly, 'you'll come back yere, and I'll get something ready.'

'Thanks Mair, but I don't think I can cope with any more of this idiot today,' Desmond playfully cuffed Neil on the back of his head.

'Watch my 'air you, it took me ages to get it like this, this morning.'

'Well if you get yere before three, you'll be alright. He doesn't get back from the pub until then,' said Mair.

'Come on, let's get out of this madhouse,' Amanda said flatly, as they made their way towards the door.

'Going tiger hunting are you?' Neil shouted when Amanda and Desmond were in the passage way.

'There aren't any tigers in Jamaica,' Desmond shouted back, 'not even in Africa. There are lions in Africa. Tigers are from China or India.'

'I'm warning you,' they heard Mair say as they went through the door.

'Well, it's a lovely day,' Desmond said once outside the house.

'I know, fab. I was extra pleased when I saw it this morning.'

They walked side by side down the street. The morning was as bright and fresh as the cold milk Amanda had poured on her cereal that morning, but eaten little of. There was the sound of birds preparing for the day ahead. They passed two women, standing talking on a doorstop, a few doors along, arms folded across their chests like car bumpers. They fell silent on seeing Amanda and Desmond approach.

'Good morning,' Desmond acknowledged them.

'Good morning,' one of the women replied without smiling.

They took the next corner, at a gap between the houses in the street, and turned into a narrow alley between the blocks of terraces. Lines of drying materials were strung between posts in the back gardens. Bedsheets, knitted jumpers, socks and colourful towels. Once out of the alley, they walked down the sloping streets, and Desmond became bewildered as they turned left onto another slope, which took them down between the intersections of five other streets. They left the right angles of the streets, and the sideways glances of shoppers behind them, to cross a main road. There was a combination of aromas, such as hot tarmac, car fumes and baking bread. They took a bridge across the river. A river which had carved its way, and now slithered through the villages of Aedre like a slippery snake.

'What's going on here then?' Desmond pointed to steel baskets upended in the river. 'A place where shopping trollies go to die?'

'Oh, I know,' Amanda said disapprovingly, 'people take them to where their car is parked, and just leave them there. Many a drunkard on a Friday and Saturday night, 'as great fun, pushing each other around in them. Then they throw them in the river.'

Across the river was an industrial wasteland, that interrupted the houses from the mountains. A large tract of unoccupied land. Crumbling edifices coated in grime. Buildings long since fallen into decay from inattention, along with the decline of the mining industry. They passed windows now devoid of glass. A place where once stone, steel, rust and revolution had gathered. Now there were just relics of former industrial prowess and glory, long since lost. Graffiti was now the only decoration, amongst a debris of rusted cans, sheets of abandoned corrugated iron, tangles of cable and barbed wire. Collapsed buildings bearing testimony to an industry that once flourished in the area. A graveyard for once unblemished hope. Now desperate pieces of land, left to rust.

'We call this the dead zone,' Amanda said.

'What was once here?'

'Factories. At five o'clock this place used to be buzzing. My mother used to work yere. In the cafeteria. Loads of my friend's parents used to work yere.'

'What happened?'

'Don't know,' Amanda shrugged her shoulders, 'they just closed down.'

'What did the workers do?'

'Don't know. Some of them went to other factories, or found work outside the villages of Aedre. Not straight away. Many were out of work for a long time. My friend Kathy, after being out of work for eight months, did GCSEs in the tech, and even an A-level. She got a job as a receptionist at a doctor's'

'All this land going to waste. They could do something here. A sports centre, or even if only clearing the place, and grassing it over.'

They walked over a divided slabbed mass of concrete. Ocean plates, with slashes of green between the divides. Clutches of weed sprouting through broken tarmac. Here was a green area, at the edge of the vast, useless worn piece of space. Grass made bald by chemical leach. Elements of coal, released into the air, like escaped prisoners on the run, to criminally cultivate acid rain. A discarded, blackened hulk of a burnt-out car, sat in the middle of the green expanse, as if it had surrendered and accepted defeat. Lost its purpose like the fallen buildings alongside. They were ankle deep in grass now. Getting small electric shocks from the stemless thistles, they were carefully picking their way though. An orchard of nettles which became progressively denser and taller, until they had to battle their way through brambles. Thorn bushes of barbed wire, as impenetrable as that dividing war zones. Eventually the land rose and swelled back to grass.

'Thank goodness for that,' Desmond gasped between heavy breaths. 'I know you warned me the mountains were steep, but I didn't expect a triathlon obstacle course. I think I rather *would* hunt tigers.'

'We 'aven't started yet,' Amanda smiled with a wicked glint in her eye.

'You mean that was just the warm up?!'

They reached a plateau, which was flattened to make way for a road, which they crossed. Desmond was relieved to see a tarmac path, on the next stage of the mountain across the road. The path was screened by uniform conifers. They passed a former collier owner's house, which appeared like a mansion from a Daphne du Maurier novel. The front wall was lower than the back. The land became lost in the trees. Domesticated forests of intense green extended up the sides of the mountain.

'These are not native to these parts,' Desmond commented, 'I'm expecting to turn a corner, and come across a little wooden house that makes Toblerones.'

'They've been yere as far back as I can remember. My father took me and Neil out yere once, when I was little, and he got lost.'

'What, and he was born here!'

'When we got 'ome my mother said, "Where 'ave you been?! I was about to send out a search party." "You wouldn't recognise the place now," he said, "all trees 'ave been planted. It's like a maze."'

The ascending road suddenly lost its tarmacked smoothness, and turned into rubble, small stones and earth lumps, shed by the cut sides of the mountain. Similar to skins shed by snakes that slunk through the mountain grasses. The sides of the mountain verges were crumbling. The effects of road building many years ago. Built for mountain vehicles needing access to the forestry. The ground bore the crenelated tracks of a heavy vehicle. The light through the trees cast meshed patterns all around them. The sun describing shadows across the asphalt. There were paths, trodden through leaf litter, leading through other parts of the forest, but there was little light there. A few plants, but only those able to tolerate shade, or fungus which thrived on decay. Parts of the inland forest had been touched only by spiders. On peering into the darkness Desmond noticed a spider had spun an elaborate web between two slim trunks, hoping to capture anything curious enough to enter. Desmond breathed in the warm air, the morning had been good to them, the sun bled over some large dew drenched rocks, along the side of the rugged track. Rocks too large to be moved, had been buffed and polished by years of rain. Some bore the scars of machinery. The intermittent sound of traffic from the road they had crossed, was now a hiss like that emitted between radio stations. They caught an aromatic and resinous scent, which reminded Amanda of her mother's bathroom on a Saturday morning. They walked slower now, savouring the musk emanating from the trees.

The path left the shadows of hovering pine trees, and Amanda looked at Desmond's long, stretched shadow as they walked. The mountain parted and tilted to form a ditch through which ran a stream, making its way to the river. They walked alongside this tinkling stream, following its counter flow. They stopped to listen to the soporific sound of this babbling brook, and caught sight of what at first looked like a black insect crawling down the mountain. Then arms and legs appeared, turning into a matchstick figure, which morphed into a human. As the human came closer and closer, they could discern it was a man. The man was in his sixties, with a wide, fast-paced gait. He carried a walking stick, which he did not seem to need, so it just swung along beside him, with the rhythm of his walk.

'Alright love?' He slowed down, and looked at Amanda with concern.

'Yes, I'm fine thanks,' Amanda smiled at him, as he walked past.

'Hasn't he seen a black man before,' Desmond said with amusement.

'You've created a myth now,' Amanda raised her eyebrows, 'There is a monster living in a cave up yere.'

'Just as well he didn't use that weapon he was swinging, on me.'

'He probably thought you 'ad a spear nearby.'

They continued their ascent, chuckling. A few yards ahead, the track become lost to sight, and the ground was softer and more yielding. Roots of trees emerged from the ground like chicken claws. The mountain at the side of them was much steeper, practically perpendicular. A path had been made by flattened grass. Trees bending one way as if begging to the sun, unevenly shaped by decades of howling wind.

'I'm sure this walk was meant for mountain goats,' Desmond panted, half way up the unforgiving slope.

On reaching the top of the mountain however, a different world awaited to greet them. A small group of sheep ran away on seeing their approach. They were met by an expanse of gorse and fern. It was like an explosion of verdant splendour. They could now see the massed pines, stretching over the mountain slopes below them. Plants waiting to be pollinated. Purple trumpets of foxgloves, dandelions and daisies packed so closely together they resembled bristles of a broom. Even the temperature was different, and Desmond's cheeks were stung by the cold air. He stood still, mouth slack with awe, breath quick as he surveyed fields clouded with clover; bushes studded with berries. A season of growth was before them. A landscape that could not be domesticated. Their chests heaved as they filled their lungs with air.

'It's a green desert up here,' he breathed to the impressive panorama.

The wind brushed around them, as if wanting to make itself known. Reminding them which part of the season they were in. The wind was a fountain, giving out tumbling fresh air. Desmond shivered along with the rippling ferns, and ran his fingers down the serrated edges of his jacket.

'It's cold up here,' he zipped up his jacket.

'What?! The sun is out in full bloom.'

'Yeah, but it's a heatless sun. My father used to say you had a naughty sun. The sun would get into his eyes. It never did that in Jamaica he used to say.'

'Get out, sun is sun innit. Let's sit down over there, where it will not be so cold.'

They found a patch of ground which had been warmed by the sun, and sucked in the cool bright day, until their breath returned to its natural rhythm. The dew had now dried and the breeze drifted the fresh scent of fern over them. Surrounding flowers also exuded a sweet gas. Here was a menu for the senses, of sight, sound, smell, and they fed on the feast provided. Nature was overflowing in the form of flora, fauna and geology. Glaciers long since vanished, had once pushed through the village, leaving green mountain walls. It's imprint, an infrastructure for the roads which were subsequently built. There had been little sign of mankind for the last ten minutes of their walk, apart from an abandoned lager can. Some ginger-coloured ants crawled over a patch of bald earth near them. Observed from this elevation, the mountains, which could be so intimidating to the uninitiated, had the capacity to turn people into shrunken humans, and sheep into white dots.

'Shows humans for what we really are,' Desmond murmured slowly, as if mesmerised. 'Little insignificant people. It's like looking at life under a microscope.'

'What are we?' Amanda murmured back in reply. 'Just a road going through mountains. Not like Casteldaeg.'

'Yeah, we have lots of roads, and no mountains. Here is beauty and simplicity. The villagers here talk of their mountains. But the villages belong to the mountains, not the other way around.'

'Villagers,' Amanda said derisively, 'you make us sound like something out of the *Beverly Hillbillies*.'

'You are gifted with glorious green,' Desmond continued unperturbed. 'These careless expanses of tree-filled land. You're lucky, I return to the world of cars, smog and pollution. These mountains would once have been mightier, but are now worn by erosion. What kind of fossils do they have in Aedre?'

'I don't know,' Amanda said in a voice which suggested he had asked her how to build a rocket to get to the moon.

'I bet these mountains conceal many stories. What once swarmed beneath this ground?' he asked rhetorically. 'I'll have to look in the museum.'

'I 'aven't been there since school!'

'What's that little village over there?' Desmond pointed to a small settlement, snuggled into a craggy basin, at the bottom of the mountain, like a cat curled up in front of a log fire, protected by the surrounding mountains.'

'That's Combfeld.'

The sides of the mountain were congested with rows of stone houses. Reassuringly solid and sensible. Multiple terraces, essays in local stone and slate. Tributaries of little roads that twisted and weaved around the streets.

'Imagine living in one of those houses down there,' Desmond indicated the first row of houses, right at the bottom of the opposite mountain.

'I don't want to. That's Miners Row. The first houses to be built in Aedre apparently. They look it too, pokey.'

'But imagine opening your curtains to that view each morning.'

'I'd rather not thank you.'

'What would you want to see then?' Desmond asked sceptically.

'Something 'appening.'

'Like muggings and stabbings.'

'Why did your parents come yere?' Amanda asked softly

'They were told they were needed here, and thought they would be welcomed,' Desmond's gaze was still fixed on the view before him. 'Instead, they were looked upon as animals. Only worse. The British love their animals. They came optimistic and fighting for the future. A future to make Britain great, and to be a part of that. My mother thought she was coming to a country where ladies politely acknowledged neighbours, and sipped tea on neat lawns.' Sarcasm had crept into Desmond's voice. 'She perfected her accent, so when passing her first English lady, she said "Good morning Marm," only to be shot a poisoned look and asked, "Who the hell do you think you're talking to Nigger?"

'Why Desmond,' Amanda sat up straighter, 'that's terrible.'

'I love this space and emptiness,' Desmond lay back, supported by his elbows, intoxicated by the crisp air to which the sun had lent its warmth. 'I could spend all day in this place, which is unknown to city dwellers. Just listening to the birds and cicadas.'

'What on earth are cicadas when they're at 'ome? Sounds like a cocktail off a Spanish menu.'

'Like grasshoppers,' Desmond chuckled.

The silence again became delicate. They were away from man-made noise.

'Do you 'ave a girlfriend Desmond?' Amanda asked shyly.

Desmond shook his head with quick short movements.

''Ave you ever 'ad one?'

'Yes, I did have one.'

'What 'appened to her.'

'She left me for someone else.'

'Oh, I'm so sorry.'

'It's OK.'

Desmond studied Amanda's face, looking at her from his semi recumbent position. 'I'm going to say something to you now, which may offend you,' he spoke gently.

'Go ahead,' Amanda tried not to sound curious, but sat a little taller.

'I think you'd look better without makeup.'

'I work in a nail salon,' Amanda shook her head.

'Yes, but you don't have to wear it all the time,' Desmond said through his wide smile. 'I mean who wears makeup to walk up a mountain?'

'I look awful without it.'

'Let me be a judge of that, and I'm a good judge of beauty. Besides, I can't imagine you looking awful.'

'Well I do, so come on,' she said playfully, 'let's get a move on.' She stood up, grabbed his arm, and pulled him up, fortified by a closeness between them.

Small boundary walls, thrown up from loose local rocks and stones, wandered all over the mountain.

'It's amazing these walls are still standing,' Desmond said, 'as they have no binding material. They must have been very skilful, to build something like this, that could withstand all the wind and rain you get here.'

Some of the dry-stone walls which they passed, were painted green with lichen.

'That shows there is no pollution,' Desmond pointed to the lichen. 'You won't see lichen growing in Casteldaeg.'

'There's plenty of pollution in the pubs around yere on the weekend. Do you go with Neil and the crowd to the Drag after work on a Friday?'

'The Green Dragon? Not if I can avoid it.'

'I don't know 'ow you stick it in there. Fighting your way through all that smoke.'

'What's your hangout then?'

'The Falstaff, or the Futures as we call it. It's not too bad.'

'That's where it all happens then, is it? The main scene.' Desmond gave a bemused smile, showing his porcelain white teeth.

'That's where anybody who's anybody around yere goes,' Amanda said with a roll of her eyes.

'I'm intrigued. You'll have to take me there.'

'Well don't expect the bright lights of Casteldaeg.'

'That's not what I want.'

'I suppose it's got to be better than the Drag.'

'That settles it then. How about next Friday.'

'OK.'

'That looks a bit alien up there,' Desmond held the flat palm of his hand above his eyes, and was looking at a transmission cable tower. A towering steel frame, which seemed to touch the edges of the clouds.

'Massive innit. I'll take you over to the stone age camp if you want to see something ancient.'

'You have a stone age camp here,' Desmond fixed an incredulous stare on Amanda.

'Don't look too shocked. There's no longer people living in them. We're not that behind the times.'

'I thought you said Miners Row were the first houses to be built in Aedre.'

Amanda pulled her face into a jibe, and led him to a number of stone piles which formed a circle. Collapsed houses, which once must have been a small hardy community. Remnants of an ancient people.

'Seems strange to think humans once lived yere. Without telephones, microwaves and videos. Not realising there was an America and a France,' Amanda mused.

'The sun was their God.'

'I wonder what they thought rain was then? They must 'ave seen a lot of it up yere. Did they think their God had abandoned them? My friend's father who plays golf. Whenever he gets up on a Saturday morning, when there is a tournament or something going on, and he looks out the window, and it is emptying down with rain, says, "There's no God."'

'They probably would have seen me as an invader. Even the Romans never got as far as here. You are therefore unique. An untamed race, saved from invasions and foreign influences.' The amusement had returned to his voice.

'Unique. You can say that again. Right enough of this. We can go back Combfeld way if you like, but if we don't get back soon, my mother will be sending out a search party.'

'We don't want her to think I've put you in a pot and eaten you,' Desmond grinned.

'You nutter,' Amanda punched his upper arm playfully.

They walked for a while along the flat land on top of the mountain. The air was cool and refreshing, despite the bright sun, which swam in the sky. They came to a waist high fence, made up of four parallel lines of rusted steel wire. The bottom wire had tufts of sheep wool stuck to it. A group of sheep about twenty meters behind them stood shoulder to shoulder.

'Look at those,' Desmond pointed to them. 'You don't need a Roman army here.'

'They're all over the place. They congregate around the ice cream van over there.'

'They have an ice cream van to feed the sheep?' Desmond uttered in disbelief.

'Not to feed the sheep,' Amanda scoffed, as they tentatively made their way down the sloping land. 'People stop, 'ave an ice cream, and the sheep pester them for some.'

'A day out feeding sheep. I can see your knees are better at taking the strain than mine,' Desmond said as some sheep raised their heads in unison, and watched them walk past. They walked further in the direction of the ice cream van, which Desmond thought looked out of place on the side of a mountain road. Some sheep were lying in the grass like overstuffed pillows, after a morning full of grazing on grass and ice cream.

'These sheep are veterans of the mountainside. Look,' Desmond stopped suddenly, 'there's a black one.'

'Black sheep were once prized for the colour of their wool.'

'They were given more respect than black people then.'

'Aw come on. Not everyone is against black people.'

'Wait here, I don't want to go just yet.' Desmond stood staring at the view below him again. 'Just one last look.'

He looked at the mountain opposite, which was pitted with what looked like acne scars, resembling the moons crater. Deep earth processes had worked on the accumulation of plants over hundreds and thousands of years, to be transformed to coal. Now all that was left were just ungrateful patches of land, where nothing but grass could grow. The village, daunted by the mountain. The straight indistinguishable terraces of houses, lining the steep mountain. Civilisation had imposed pragmatic shapes, and parts of the mountain had been flattened.

They continued until they reached the tarmac road of the Sceard, which they walked alongside, accompanied by the grind of gears from heavy vehicles, changing down to their lowest. The breath of the late morning wind was now shallower. They were back again at Amanda's house which smelt pleasantly of baking.

'You're back,' Mair came from the kitchen in an apron. 'I was beginning to wonder if you'd got lost. I've made some welsh cakes.'

'That's what that delicious smell is,' Desmond flashed his alluring grin.

'I've also made some stew, so sit down, you must be 'ungry after all that walking.'

'She doesn't go to all this effort for us,' Neil looked up from his paper, which he was reading from an armchair.

'You're not down the pub then?' Amanda said with mock irony.

'Give us a chance, I've not long got up. Went back to bed, didn't I.'

'Now why doesn't that surprise me.'

'What's happening in the world mate?' Desmond's grin had not left his face.

'No use asking him,' Wayne came into the room. 'He doesn't know what's happening outside his own door. He only reads the sports pages.'

'Well it's better than reading all this economy trash. Shares going up and down. The only share I've got is what you'll share with me.'

'That's my aftershave, shirts and newspaper, so give it here.'

'No wonder he hasn't got a girlfriend,' Desmond laughed.

'Neither 'ave you,' Neil said sourly.

Amanda quickly picked up a magazine, which she rifled through.

'How about you Wayne?' Desmond turned his attention to the other brother, 'is there a special lady in your life?'

'Under the thumb 'im mate,' Neil stabbed the thumb of his closed fist to the ground. 'She's got a ring on her finger. Anita, I need 'er too,' Neil teased.

'You're engaged, are you? Congratulations. How did you two meet?'

'At a union meeting. She works in the offices of a factory down Briog.'

'Another politician,' Neil said with irony. 'Conversation must be riveting.'

'I wish they'd both 'urry up and get married,' Mair shouted from the kitchen.

'It's a bloody disgrace,' Gerald came in from the garden via the kitchen. 'No responsibility. In my day most men were married, or at least engaged by the time they got to twenty-one.'

'Yere we go again,' Neil raised his eyebrows to the ceiling. 'He'll be mentioning the war next.'

'They want, want, want these days,' Gerald continued. 'In my day we didn't 'ave two ha'pennies to rub together.'

'Why would you want to rub them together?' Amanda asked indignantly.

'Your dinners on the table,' Mair walked to the dining area, carrying dishes with a tea towel.

'And less cheek from you an all,' Gerald pointed towards Amanda, who shrugged as soon as he looked away, palms facing upwards, mouth open.

'With your cooking Mair, is it any wonder they don't want to get married,' Desmond said whilst they all took a seat at the table.

Desmond spoke of the walk he and Amanda had taken that morning, between mouthfuls of food. Telling them how lucky they were to be living in such a place. 'She took me to see the sacred ground.'

'What, Casteldaeg Arms Field?' joked Neil.

'Now that's just the type of unintelligent comment, I would expect from you,' Amanda said, shaking her head. 'I see the rugby fans passing the salon on match days. I said to Abigail, "It's only ten o'clock. They're not playing until two." "Aw come on," she said, "they'll be in the pub won't they?"'

'Nothing wrong with that,' said Neil.

Desmond offered to help carry the dishes to the kitchen once the meal was finished, at which Mair flapped her hands and told him to sit down.

'Well I won't impose on your hospitality any longer,' Desmond looked at his watch. 'Thank you again Mair for a wonderful meal,' he shouted to the kitchen.

'Oh, it was nothing,' came the returning voice. 'Anytime.'

He made his way to the door, followed by Amanda.

'Thank you for a wonderful morning,' Desmond said, looking straight into Amanda's eyes with a searching expression. 'What an amazing place this is. I look forward to going to the Futures pub next Friday.'

'Don't get too excited,' Amanda's mouth felt dry. 'It's not exactly the Hacienda.'

'Anything will be wonderful with you,' he said softly.

He brushed her left cheek with the backs of his fingers, barely touching her skin. 'Thank you and goodbye,' he said, as he moved to his car.

'Bye', she raised her right hand in a wave, and watched him drive out of view. The nerve endings of her left cheek tingled, as she listened to the sound of his car getting fainter and fainter.

Chapter 3

Amanda lavishly sprinkled the rapidly filling bath tub with liquid foam, as if preparing a bath for a god. She watched the mountains of froth form like a snow scene. Neil has been in here, she had thought on entering the room, due to the aroma of the shampoo he used, that smelt of chewing gum. She smothered her face with moisturiser, which she had taken from the collection of tubs and bottles, that vied for space on the set of three bathroom shelves. She tentatively dipped a toe into the bath water, before removing her bath robe, and slowly lowered the rest of herself into the rewarding warmth of the scented water. She relaxed her back against the warm plastic of the bath. The room was now milky with steam, cascading in swirls, which Amanda watched through half-closed eyes. The steamed air was scented with cherry blossom.

Amanda gave a cat like stretch, as her limbs loosened, and her muscles went slack. She was drowsy with the vapours floating around the small room. She rested her head on the rim of the bath, and thought dreamily back to last Saturday, and her walk with Desmond to the top of the mountain. She was transported back to that garden of Eden, amongst the trees and flowers. She mused over how he had looked at her, through his molten brown eyes. He had looked at her in a way that had made her feel prized. How different he was to other boys she had known. Boys who put on an act of bravado. As if they didn't care about anything. It was cool not to care. They feared that to show emotions was unmasculine. Even Nigel, whom she had known since childhood, acted differently when he was with his mates. She recalled how Desmond had spoken about the things his mother had gone through, when she first came to Britain. Desmond had no such hang ups about his masculinity. She was jolted from her rapture by a rap on the wood of the door.

'Bloody hurry up in there,' Wayne shouted. 'You've been in there almost an hour. Other people live here as well, you know.'

'Urry up and marry Anita then, if things are that bad. I'll be out now.'

The water now felt tepid, and the steam had turned into condensation, which was running down the walls in rivulets. Amanda released the plug, stood upright, and waited a few seconds for the water to fall from her, before wrapping a towel around herself. She shivered a little, as she stepped out of the bath, but felt a stimulating shock of cold water from the wash basin, as she splashed water on her face, to remove any remaining traces of unabsorbed moisturiser. She patted the rest of herself dry, with the towel, before putting her bath robe back on. She moved from the bathroom to her bedroom, and pulled from the wardrobe the clothes she would wear that night. These were a pair of black and mostly white check trousers, with a thread of pink and grey. A pink, round neck jumper, the neck of which came to just under her throat. She put a CD into the player, and the room filled with the energetic vibe of techno music. She looked into the mirror to apply lipstick, after which she rubbed her browned lips together. She heard the doorbell ring as she was deciding which chunky gold chain to wear around her neck. She turned off the music and heard Wayne invite Desmond into the sitting room.

'Where you off tonight then?' she could hear voices, but her hearing had to compete with the sound of the television drifting up the stairs.

'The Futures! More like lack of futures... Anybody over twenty-one there mate, is old.'

'Wow, you look fabulous,' Desmond exclaimed as Amanda walked into the room. Her teeth were brushed, face washed, hair carefully combed to one side, she had slipped on a pair of black loafers, so was now fully dressed.

Gerald tutted from his armchair in front of the television. 'She looks like a clown with all that makeup and check trousers.'

'Thanks,' she stammered to Desmond, as her eyes locked onto him, and she struggled to find words. He looked amazing. He wore a burgundy tailored shirt, over slim black trousers, with shiny, smart black lace-up shoes. He laughed, bemused by her reaction. Mair, who was normally watching television at this time, had been happily chatting to Desmond.

'You didn't tell me Desmond was coming tonight,' she said slightly admonishingly. 'I would 'ave made 'im something to eat.'

'He 'as a mother who cooks Mam.'

'Your mother kindly offered me some food, but I've already had a big meal. Where's Neil?'

'Need you ask?' Amanda said derisively, 'He's down the pub, in' he.'

'Well he has to get to the bathroom before you, doesn't he?' said Wayne.

'We'd better get going,' Desmond laughed.

They left Mair and Gerald in the irradiated glow from the television, and Wayne who was taking the stairs three at a time. Before leaving the house, they heard Mair shouting up to Wayne, 'Ave you 'ad enough to eat?'

'Of course, you saw me eat at teatime,' came the reply.

Amanda noticed the twitching of curtains from behind downstairs windows, out of the corner of her eye, as they made their way down the street.

'Ello Mrs Morris,' Amanda said to a woman putting a key into the lock of a door. The woman turned and gave a fraudulent smile.

They walked past the cinema and library. Buildings which announced that particular part of the village as being one of importance. The assertive architecture of the cinema, which had been built years ago, as a place of entertainment for the miners.

'I'll take you to the Social first,' Amanda said.

'What's the Social?' Desmond asked with puzzlement.

'Everybody goes to one of them first. They're old men's clubs, but the drinks are cheap.'

They walked jauntily along the main road. The air was warm between the houses and shops lining the road, the light was peachy. The sun was just hovering on the mountain line, casting an orange gold warmth over the village.

'This road is quiet,' Desmond remarked. 'There were loads of cars here last Saturday. It was busy all the way back to Casteldaeg.'

'It's usually quiet in the evenings.'

Their shoes crunched over cubes of shattered glass, which lay strewn across the pavement, from a kicked in bus shelter. Amanda noticed the tone in people's eyes as they walked past.

'Haven't you seen a black man before?' Desmond sneeringly asked a group of four staring young people.

'Yes, we 'ave black sheep yere, and they've got more sense than you.'

Amanda could feel the blood burning over her face. 'Take no notice of them,' she said angrily. 'Stupid prats, you could crush 'im between your fingers. He wouldn't 'ave said anything if he'd been on his own. He's only a dwt.'

'He's a what!' Desmond said through a bemused grin.

'A dwt, you know, a little person.'

'You have your own language here. What did someone at the factory say the other day. "He's always wearing daps."'

'Daps, aye, you know, canvas things you do sport in.'

'Plimsolls. He was talking about plimsolls! You do sport in trainers. You could pull a tendon running in plimsolls.'

'Plimsolls,' Amanda scoffed, 'sounds like something out of a St Trinian's book.'

'There was an African athlete who could only run barefoot. He was made to wear trainers, but took them off when he was losing a big race. Then he went speeding past the others. There are many villages in Africa where kids are lucky to have any form of shoe.'

'Let's cross over,' Amanda said on seeing a gang of teenage boys coming towards them.

'It'll be ok. We'll only make it worse if they think we're scared.'

Amanda stared straight ahead on walking past them.

'Why don't you get back to yer own country?' one of them shouted as soon as they had passed.

Desmond turned to face them.

'I was born here. Where do you expect me to go back to boys?'

'Back to the jungle, coloured man.'

Amanda went rigid as Desmond walked up to them, and stopped a few steps in front of them.

'When I'm ill, I'm black,' Desmond said calmly. 'When I'm angry, I'm black. When I'm cold, I'm black. When I'm scared, I'm black.' He paused, and held their stare for a few seconds, at which they shifted uncomfortably. 'When you're ill, you're yellow. When you're angry, you're red. When you're cold, you're blue. When you're scared, you're white. So why are you boys calling me coloured?'*

The youths just stared at him, but said nothing. Desmond walked backwards for three steps, before turning and walking back to Amanda, who stood with chest and shoulders heaving with quick breaths.

'Smartass Nigger,' one of the youths shouted, once there was some distance between them.

Desmond ignored the taunt. Amanda felt as if she had grown taller as she hooked onto Desmond's arm. Her shoulders were thrust back, chin slightly raised as she guided him down a side street.

'Yere's the Social,' she said, before a large square building, amongst a row of terraced houses.

'Here!' Desmond said in disbelief. 'I bet the residents love this place. Raucous people coming out of here late at night.'

'Not that type of place.'

Four wide steps led to a massive hollow square entrance, before a thick glass double door. The glass of which, was made

---

* Quote from unknown source

up of reinforced wire. Inside was a bare corridor with two side doors and a staircase. The air smelt of a combination of wood polish, hops and cigarette smoke. It was not an overwhelming smell however. They went through one of the side doors to a large lounge. There was a rich red carpet covering the floor. The walls were of pink and grey flock wall paper. Apart from which, there was that lack of décor, which made all working men's clubs look the same. Groups of men in their sixties to eighties, dressed in thick tweed jackets and flat caps sat around tables, with pint glasses of brown liquid in front of them, inhaling cigarettes.

Desmond felt their eyes on him, beaming contempt. Three men in their thirties stood at the end of the bar, who apart from a glance, displayed no interest. Groups of girls in their late teens, early twenties, and young couples sat at other tables amongst the groups of older men. The younger ones were dressed as if they were going to a night club. One group of girls were drinking from pint glasses through a straw. These groups looked at Desmond with curiosity more than contempt, trying not to stare, but finding it difficult.

Desmond stood at the bar waiting to be served. The bartender ignored him, as if hoping he would disappear. A stain on his club.

'Any chance of being served?' Desmond said loudly, 'I have money you know.'

'We don't serve your sort around yere,' the bartender glanced at him, then went straight back to pulling the tap in front of him. The bartender was large, round, bald and had a flushed pink face.

'And what sort would that be?' Desmond asked, with a hint of menace in his voice.

'You know what I mean,' the bartender put down the pint glass he was filling, stood squarely before Desmond with his palms on the counter. 'I don't want any jiggaboos in my club.'

Amanda inhaled sharply.

'Do you mean black people?' Desmond enquired with practiced calmness. 'Cause I don't see any signs for no coloureds.

44

Does that mean coloureds are allowed then? Cause I don't see no sign saying otherwise.' Desmond's eyebrows were raised.

'Leave 'im alone,' one of the girls from a corner of the lounge, shouted to the barman, as she raised a pint glass to her rouged lips.

'Now don't you get clever with me son,' the bartender pointed a finger at Desmond.

'You're my father, are you? I'll have to speak to my mother about that.'

The trio of men at the bar sniggered.

'I'm warning you,' the bartender now flushed with red, rushed from behind the bar, and stood before Desmond, looking up into his face.

'We fought two world wars for this country, and it was not for the likes of you,' shouted a man in his seventies, sitting in a group, his hands on the top of his walking stick.

'Black men also fought in both world wars,' Desmond looked over to the speaker. 'Britain recruited 600,000 black men to fight for this country. Many African Americans died in World War Two.'

One of the trio at the bar started singing 'Buffalo Solider' quietly, but audible enough to be heard by those close by.

'Do you know what a Buffalo soldier is boys?' Desmond turned to face the trio, who looked awkwardly down into their drinks.

'Buffalo soldiers were African Americans, whose task it was to control the Native Americans. A race who had suffered the same discrimination, exploitation and subjugation as themselves.'

'That's it now,' the barman again pointed at Desmond. 'I've 'ad enough of you, coming in yere causing trouble. You leave NOW.'

'Well, I will say goodnight to all you people and your village hospitality,' Desmond took a step away from the bartender, and half turned to the rest of the lounge. 'Your village hospitality, which I've heard so much about,' his voice now heaving with sarcasm.

'I'll buy you a drink,' a girl of about eighteen stood up, opening her purse.

'No. Thank you for offering, lovely lady, but I won't outstay my welcome. And I thought segregation went out in fifties America.' Desmond sneered at the bartender as he turned and walked to the door, which he opened to let Amanda walk through. Amanda however stopped before the door.

'What's your problem?' Amanda addressed the lounge. 'He harms no one. He is a lovely person and works 'ard. He's not scrounging on the dole like some around yere.'

'Don't you start now,' the bartender wagged his finger at her. 'I run this bar.' He jabbed his thumb towards his chest. 'I decide who comes in yere, and if you don't like it, you can go somewhere else.'

'Don't worry, I will,' Amanda replied.

'So that was my introduction to the Social,' Desmond let out a long, slow breath, as soon as they were outside. The day was turning into twilight. That time when it was not possible to discern colour.

'I'm sorry,' Amanda said dolefully, her hands by her sides.

'Don't worry, people can't help their ignorance.'

They walked back to the main road.

'My father used to tell me, when he was a boy, these streets were throbbing and pulsing at the end of a coal shift. Look at them now,' Amanda said melancholily.

'Don't knock it. We have the streets to ourselves for a while. At least, until the next person starts giving me hassle'.

'Oh why are people such idiots,' Amanda said almost pleadingly.

'That's just the way things are. Let's not let them spoil our night.' He put his arm around her shoulders, and the bounce entered their stride once more. They passed some houses on the side of the road, which were grander than the other terraced houses. The terraced houses that lacked ornamentation, apart from some coloured paint around the windows and different types of doors. These houses had some intricate wrought iron trellising.

'They are my favourite 'ouses,' Amanda pointed at them.

'Reminds me of Jamaica.'

'Ave you been there?' Amanda's eyes were opened wide.

'Nah, but I'd love to. I've seen pictures of it. My father would love to go back there one day. There's some rough parts to it. Big difference between the wealthy and the poor. The wealthy don't venture into the poorer areas, and if those from the rough areas are seen in the wealthy neighbourhood, they are stopped by the police.'

Ivy clung to the walls of the end house, like soot clinging to the skin of a miner. The shadowy curtain of dusk was gradually beginning to block out the rest of the daylight.

'Well, yere we are,' Amanda said with a note of satisfaction, after another twenty minutes of walking. They stood outside a square building, with a slab like awning over the door, supported by two thick pillars.

'Welcome to the Futures pub.'

A colourful sign labelled Falstaff hung high on the edge of the building, with a portrait of the Shakespearean character, looking like the Laughing Cavalier. There were three upper windows on the façade of the building, and two larger lower windows either side of the pillars. A bouncer dressed in what amounted to smartness, which was an open necked navy-blue polo shirt, and black trousers acknowledged them with a nod and a good evening, but made no attempt to open the large double doors of the entrance for them. He was over six feet tall, well built, with close cropped dark brown hair. His sense of importance made him seem taller. Desmond who was as tall as him returned his acknowledgement, but the bouncer did not give any further response or eye contact, just stared straight ahead. Amanda pushed the door open to a thrum of light and voices. There was the acrid tang of lager in the air, mingled with colognes and perfumes. They entered a door on their left, into the lounge, and made their way through the crush of bodies to the direction of the bar. There were groups of young people in their teens to early twenties sitting around tables, or standing in whatever space they could find.

'What are you having?' Desmond asked loudly.

'Well hello,' said a girl around Amanda's age, with voluminous dyed blonde shoulder-length hair. Her dark pink lip-sticked lips were pressed into a playful smile.

'Oh, hi Melissa.'

'Who's the new beau then?' Melissa asked, whilst Desmond battled his way to the bar.

'He works with Neil, and wanted to come yere. Goodness knows why.'

'Ah,' she said slowly, lowering her chin and widening her eyes, as if she had just made sense of some theory. 'So, you're not going out together then?'

'Well not at the moment,' Amanda said a little defensively, as she glanced at the floor, but could only see Melissa's cream, wide-legged trousers.

'But you're working on it,' Melissa said teasingly.

'Whew I finally got served,' Desmond handed Amanda a glass of white wine.

'You have to fight to get to the bar in here,' Melissa smiled.

'This is Melissa,' Amanda said as quietly as she could. She noticed the dark red polish on Melissa's fingernails.

'I'm Desmond,' he proffered his free hand to Melissa, 'pleased to meet you Melissa.'

'And I you,' Melissa said looking directly into his eyes. 'Welcome to the Futures.'

'That's a rather bright top you're wearing,' Desmond said looking at the bold green patterned baggy blouse.

'Well, I like to stand out, me,' she looked at Amanda with a mischievous smile. 'Add some colour to the place.'

'Oh, yere's Hannah,' Amanda grabbed hold of the arm of another girl of around her age. 'Hannah lives about two streets in front of me. Desmond works with Neil, we walked up Cotlif mountain last week.'

'How did far did you go,' Hannah said matter of factly.

'To the top, and back down the Sceard.'

'The top,' Hannah exclaimed, 'what are you trying to do to the boy?'

'He can handle it,' the devious smile had returned to Melissa's face.

Desmond lowered his head towards Hannah, and continued a conversation, which required some lip-reading.

'Come on Melissa, your drink is getting warm,' another girl appeared from the crowd, with aggressively bleached hair.

'Sexy, stylish, and a little different. I like that,' Melissa said quietly to Amanda, before she followed the girl back to a table.

Hannah was mouthing and exaggerating her syllables, as if speaking to a five-year-old.

'It's OK love,' Desmond said, 'I can speak English.'

A pink flush crept over Hannah's cheeks.

'Got a cancer stick?' asked a skinny male of about eighteen. He was shorter than Hannah, with acne eruptions all over his face. She immediately became preoccupied with searching the bag at her hip.

'I can see them there,' the boy pointed to the white packet in her bag.

'I was wondering if I'd see you yere tonight,' another male said to Amanda. He looked the same age as her, and wore baggy jeans, with a check shirt, open to the bottom of his chest, exposing a plain white tee shirt. His light brown hair was short on the sides, with a floppy fringe. He was slim and about three inches taller than Amanda.

'Nigel,' Amanda's voice went up two octaves. 'Ow 'ave you been?' she asked enthusiastically.

'Same old, same old. Stan keeping us busy. He's got a contract on a new estate going up in Briog. So, we'll be busy with the pipework on that. I saw Wayne the other day. He asked if I would fit a new bathroom in the 'ouse he and Anita are buying. 'Ave they fixed a date yet for the wedding?'

'Nah, but now they've found an 'ouse, so we're expecting an announcement soon.'

'Well introduce us Amanda,' Desmond entered the conversation.

'Oh, what am I like,' Amanda shook her head, 'Nigel, this is Desmond. Desmond is from Casteldaeg, and he works with Neil.'

'You're from Casteldaeg, and you're yere tonight!' Nigel said with an expression of mock disbelief.

'I like it here,' Desmond said jovially. 'Amanda kindly took me up the mountain last Saturday. It was wonderful.'

'Did she now?' Nigel smiled and gave Amanda a knowing look.

'I don't know about that,' Amanda said without commitment, and proceeded to tell Nigel about the previous event at the Social.

'Don is such a Neanderthal,' Nigel said shaking his head. 'We're still evolving up yere mate,' he said to Desmond. 'We 'aven't accepted other races yet, but we're getting there.'

'I think you have a long way to go,' Desmond replied. 'I haven't seen a black face since I've been here. Even the beers are pale.'

'Nobody drinks anything but lager yere mate,' Nigel said, 'but yeah, you are right, we don't get that many non-whites around yere. I suppose there are better places to live. We had two Arabian students lodge yere once. The women went wild over them. Didn't last long though. I guess they moved nearer to the action.'

'There are some Chinese and Indians,' Amanda said deferentially.

'Yeah, but still not that many. Anyway, I best get back, before Archie buys the next round.'

'He fancies you,' Desmond said, as soon as Nigel had left them.

'Go on with you. Me and Nigel 'ave known each other since infants. He's seen me get stuck up trees, with chocolate stuck all over my face. I've seen 'im crying after his mother shouted at 'im.'

'I'm telling you,' Desmond insisted, 'he fancies you.'

'People are leaving now, so we can get a seat.'

'Awright Butt? A man in his early twenties acknowledged Desmond as he followed Amanda to a seat.'

'Yes, I'm OK, how are you?'

'Aye, I'm fine.'

Desmond and Amanda sat shoulder to shoulder on a long, padded seat by the wall. They observed the others left in the now emptying pub. The boy who had asked for a cigarette earlier was standing alone near the opened door. Sucking on the white tube, then blowing out a long cylinder of smoke. Amanda gazed at Desmond's features. Those full lips, which could have been moulded from clay. His sculpted body, attentiveness and humour. It was as if he had moulded himself fully into her wishes and longings.

'We'd better get going ourselves,' said Desmond, 'before they throw us out. I've had enough trouble from barmen for one night, as it is. Or that charmer on the door.'

They stepped out of the brightness of the pub, into the orange, sodium glow of the street lights. A male, with blood around his mouth, was staggering and slurring near the bouncer. The bouncer was standing rigid and upright, gaze fixed straight ahead.

'He probably tried arguing with the bouncer,' Desmond laughed, when they had passed the swaying male.

'I know,' Amanda replied, 'they 'ave a bit to drink, and think they're Tarzan. I've seen boys of five feet nothing, try to pick a fight with 'im. He flicks them, and they fall on the floor, and get back up still mouthing off at 'im! "Come on 'en, come on,"' Amanda adopted a pugilistic pose. 'He lets them do that twice, then he just goes up and bops them one. Often, we've 'ad to step over someone flat out on the floor.'

They had to step aside to let a group of young women, having a raucous conversation, with bouquets of chips in their hands, walk past them.

'Goodnight ladies,' Desmond smiled at them.

'Gu'night luv,' they shouted in unison.

'Let's walk up by the side of the river,' Amanda took Desmond's arm and guided him from the road. 'That way, we'll avoid any more drunkards.'

'Just people having fun.'

The river was shimmering with black and silver. They looked up at the navy black sky, which was a spectacle of stars. Amanda's breath came out in wine-scented clouds. Walking unhurriedly, arm in arm with Desmond, there was no sense in her mind the evening would ever come to an end.

'Shall we sit here for a while?' Desmond pointed to a low wall near the side of the river.

Amanda kept hold of his arm, whilst they sat down. She could feel the strong pump of his heart against her upper arm. 'What kind of music do you like?' Desmond asked.

'I like a bit of Acid House, but I also like Prince and Madonna. How 'bout you?'

'I like Bob Marley the best. Bob was the godfather of reggae. He thought music could cure the world of racism,' he said musingly. 'My brother likes UB40. Their earlier stuff was better.'

They sat in silence for a while, as if contemplating the river.

'Look, there's a moonflower,' Desmond pointed to the reflection of the full moon bobbing on the water, 'I'd like to pick it up and give it to you.'

The magic of the moon on the water, and the warm, sweet night, seemed to melt into Desmond.

'I want you to know,' Amanda said blissfully, tongue loosened by alcohol, 'that I think you are the most wonderful person I 'ave ever known.'

'Oh, I think that's the wine talking.'

'No, it's not.'

'My life has certainly got better since meeting you,' Desmond said solemnly, gazing at the sky. 'Even though it has only been a short time. There's the plough,' he said, pointing upwards to the sky.

'Oh yeah,' Amanda said disappointedly.

'You've been so good to me. You and your family. I want to do something for you. How about coming to my house for a meal?'

'Oh Desmond, I'd love that,' Amanda said enthusiastically.

'You don't work Wednesdays, do you? I'm owed some time, so I'll ask Raymond if I can finish early this Wednesday, and pick you up at say three?'

'Yeah, that will be fine.'

'Come on then, let's get going, otherwise I could stay here all night.'

So could I, thought Amanda. She clung onto Desmond's arm tightly, as she chattered incessantly on the way back. They reached the slope of Amanda's street. Light from lower floor windows brushed small square patches of brightness over front gardens and pavements. They stopped at the gate, before the steps to Amanda's house, where Desmond's car was parked. He put his hands on her shoulders.

'Thank you for a wonderful evening,' Desmond tilted his head forward and kissed her.

Amanda felt a warmth flooding through her, and a weakness in the backs of her knees.

'I'll see you Wednesday then.'

'OK,' Amanda said breathlessly, her cheeks tingling, heart pounding as she trembled her way up the steps to her door.

Chapter 4

Amanda had been thinking a lot about Desmond since they'd last seen each other the previous Friday. Hanging around, tensely waiting for the telephone to ring. Thoughts of him flowing through her mind. The softness in his face, as he gazed at the mountain. His expressions as he bantered with Neil. His smile when talking to her friends at the Futures. He'd rung her on the Sunday, to see how she was. She felt a surge in her body at the sound of his voice. She had to control her own voice, to stop herself babbling with insipid conversation. She'd asked Neil if Desmond had ever mentioned his previous girlfriend. 'Yeah, Jean. He's mentioned her once or twice, but doesn't say much about her.' Over the next two days, she found herself daydreaming. She imagined them getting married, and the beautiful coffee-coloured children they would have. Life would be different in Casteldaeg. Should not be too difficult for her to get a job there. Otherwise, she could travel to work with Desmond every morning. That way, she would see more of him, or maybe they would move to Jamaica, and live near the sea. She imagined stepping outside their house every morning, listening to the crashing waves. Air laden with sea spray.

'Gosh, these roads are narrow,' Desmond swerved to avoid an oncoming car.

Wednesday afternoon had finally arrived. She had been clock-watching all morning. Going back and fore to her wardrobe, agonising over what to wear. In the end, she had settled for a pair of navy-blue trousers, with a black and white horizontally striped, square necked top, which she tucked into her trousers. She had checked and rechecked her hair and makeup in the mirror. She wanted to achieve that smart casual look. After all, she did not want to look as if she was going to a disco, on meeting his family for the first time. Desmond was wearing a fresh pair of jeans and shirt, which he must have changed into at work.

'Yeah, Joyriders like to test their skills around the streets in the night,' said Amanda.

The narrow streets provided an obstacle course for such games.

'Bloody stupid,' Desmond replied, 'There's just enough room for one car either side. It doesn't help that there are cars parked on the road.'

The villages moved past in gold and grey majesty. The main road was the principal artery running through the villages, lined with houses, pubs and shops.

'Look at these houses either side of the road,' Desmond said with pleasant surprise. 'You could touch the next door from yours, if you stretched out your hand. So basic, no pretence at status here. I live in a terraced street. These houses are better than the shanty towns in Jamaica though. One hundred per cent. Yet you could cross a road, and there would be houses with green lawns, that looked as if they had been trimmed by a hairdresser. The white folks wanted chimneys and fireplaces in their houses.'

'Bit pointless, in an 'ot country like Jamaica innit. Is it only the white people who live in such 'ouses?'

'No, some black people have made good. Some have done really well out of tourism. Then there is gangsterism of course. There is a big divide between the rich and poor. There are some areas to be avoided. Where the Yardies operate.'

'Yardies?'

'Yeah, the rough Jamaicans.'

'Do the people from those areas ever go into the rich areas?'

'Nah, as I said last Friday, they'd be stopped by the police in minutes. They'd stick out like a sore thumb.'

They had left the villages of Aedre some time ago, and were now on the long stretch of road taking them to the city. He drove through a part of the city Amanda had never seen before.

She rarely left the nucleus of the shopping area, and she gawped in wonder, like a new-born kitten, at the wide avenues of five storey houses. The roads narrowed a little and the avenues turned into streets of terraced houses.

'Here we are then,' Desmond pulled up in front of a house, just like all the rest. There were attempts at individualism, such as brightly coloured paint around the windows and doors. 'Welcome to my humble abode.'

Amanda stood in the terraced street, which was no different from the terraces of the villages, apart from the wider road and bolder coloured doors and windowsills. This was different however. There was nobody loitering about on the street. No curtains twitching to see what car had parked and who was getting out of it.

The first sensation to hit Amanda on entering the narrow passageway of Desmond's house, was the pungent aroma. She found herself thrown into a bewildering new world of spices. A dog bounded eagerly towards her. It was dark brown, larger than a terrier, but not as large as a Labrador. The head was a bit like a Staffordshire bull terrier. He kept jumping up at her, as if trying to reach her neck.

'Bailey,' a high-pitched yet strong voice shouted from the kitchen. 'Stop that,' the voice belonged to a chuckling woman standing in the frame of the kitchen doorway.

'This is my mother Hortense,' Desmond nodded towards the heavy, but not tall woman in the doorway. Her hair was a jet-black scribble, powdered with grey, around her shining, round dark brown face. She wore a bright yellow apron, over a dark green knee length dress.

'Hello Honey.'

'Hello Mrs Brown,' Amanda said timidly. She looked around the room, which although medium sized, the amount of people and furniture made it seem smaller. The furniture were two cane sofas, with faded orange cushions, frayed at the edges. They were thinner and concave in the middle, where people had sat over the years. There was an armchair positioned to get a view of the television, which was showing cartoons. A man in his fifties sat in the chair. He was darker than Desmond, and the whites of his eyes were stark. He wore black trousers and a dark brown jacket, over a shirt with a subtle brown, green and yellow check.

'This is my father, Eugene.'

'How do you do?' Eugene extended a hand, which Amanda tentatively took.

'And this cute thing here, is my sister Shanice.'

A girl of Amanda's age sat crossed legged on a large cushion on the floor. She was taller than Amanda, slim with hair of glistening tight black curls, falling past her shoulders. She wore a white, thin sweatshirt, over a short turquoise skirt. A magazine rested in her lap, between her brown, bare, folded legs. Amanda thought she looked cool.

'Hi,' she nodded at Amanda.

'And these three devils here, are Jayde, Lloyd and Franklin.'

Three children, two boys and a girl, stood staring at Amanda, as if she were some strange species of animal at a zoo.

'Ooh, aren't they sweet?' Amanda cooed.

'Not really,' Shanice said wryly.

The smaller of the boys wore a pair of dark trousers, which seemed to hang on him, and a red jumper. He had short, closely cropped black hair, which looked as if it had been liberally painted on with black ink. The other of the boys, who seemed the elder, was about ten years old, with more flesh on him. His face was plumper and less dark, maybe his face appeared larger due to the mass of curls which framed it. He wore jeans with a dark green sweatshirt. The girl wore a pair of cerise pink leggings, with a long-sleeved mint green top, which settled half way down her thighs.

'Say hello, you rude lot,' Shanice said loudly but tonelessly.

'Aw, they're so cute,' Amanda gushed.

'These two,' Desmond pointed to the older boy and girl, 'are my brother Samuel's, and this one is my sister Annabelle's. Right, well now you've met the family, I will leave you in their capable hands whilst I take a shower. I washed as well as I could in the toilet washbasin before I left work. I won't be long.'

'Sit down love,' Eugene indicated the opposite sofa. Amanda sat down and looked at the rest of the room. There were pictures of red African suns. Red being the only vibrant colour, the rest being monotones of dark brown trees and black silhouettes of antelopes. The children sat huddled on the other sofa, trying to watch cartoons, but their gaze kept straying in Amanda's direction. Bailey had now settled on the floor beside her, and she was grateful to be able to stroke his head.

'Desmond tells me you work in a nail salon,' Shanice said, whilst flattening the magazine on the floor, ready to be put away.

'Yes, and you work in Taps.'

'That's right.'

'I love the clothes in Taps.'

'That's where I get most of mine from.'

'Do you get discount?'

'Yeah, ten per cent.'

'Handy'

'Why don't you come in here Honey. I've hardly spoken to you,' Hortense spoke from the kitchen.

Amanda made her way self-consciously to the kitchen, where she came to an abrupt stop in the doorway. The kitchen was equipped like a grocer's shop. Amanda gawped at the large bags of rice, cans and bottles containing products she had never heard of. Hortense had returned from the shops that morning, holding a bag heavy with flesh. Amanda's house had never held as much food, even at Christmas. The kitchen had an uplifting feel to it. Battered, well-used pots and pans hung from walls and cupboards. There were bold patterned ceramic tiles half way up the walls. The remainder of the walls were painted a pale yellow. The scent of exotic spices and the rich odours of simmering soups and stews was even more powerful, as if condensed into this one square of the house. Hortense was pounding spices in a mortar.

'Can I 'elp with anything?' Amanda offered, even though there was little space for them both to move around the room. Besides, she wouldn't have known what to do with the ingredients and foods she had never heard of.

'No, no Honey, you just sit yourself down there,' Hortense pointed to three stools at the side of a worktop. 'Now is there any food you don't like?' Hortense was chopping vegetables, the rap of the knife on the chopping board was steady and quick.

'Oh, I like anything me,' Amanda's breathing was now slower. 'Italian, Chinese,' she gave a little laugh. 'My mother however tends to be a plain cook. My father and brothers are none too adventurous. Egg and chips men. Wayne is not too bad. Will 'ave a takeaway, and goes to restaurants with his fiancé. My mother once tried some fancy recipe, with chicken and cream. "What the 'ell is this muck?" my father said, "Aye, I'm not too fussy an' all", said Neil,' Amanda laughed and looked at the steam rising from the saucepans.

'Well now you can try Jamaican dining. Food for Jamaicans is all about sharing the food you love, with the people you love.'

Amanda could smell cinnamon on Hortense's breath, as she leaned closely to pick up a ladle. She recognised the smell, as one her mother used to spice the cakes she made.

'Ow nice.'

'I hope you don't mind stew this time of year. Us Jamaicans never abide by protocol. We serve stew in the middle of July.'

'You haven't got her cooking now, have you mum?' Desmond appeared freshly showered and shaved on his upper jowls. He wore navy chinos and a blue check shirt.

'Oh, go on with you now,' Hortense flicked a tea towel at him. 'Tell Shanice to lay the table, and you can help me lay these plates.'

Amanda joined the others around a table, which soon became laden with food Amanda had never seen before. Chicken coated with a dark brown substance. A bowl of stew, and what looked like bananas, which they put on their plates next to some chicken. When Eugene asked for salt, all the family, even the children went for the salt cellar.

'You have some rice and peas now,' Hortense instructed Lloyd sternly, at which point he reached for the bowl of rice and red beans.

'Would you like some peppers?' Desmond asked

'Yes please,' Amanda replied, looking for a pepper pot. Desmond passed her a plate of oily looking red and green strips of vegetables. The others were passing around a small bowl of chilli seeds, which they sprinkled over their food.

The food tasted nice however. It was different to anything Amanda had ever tasted. She was expecting something like the food from Indian takeaways, but this was fresh and tasty. She kept looking towards Desmond, wanting to admire him, to adore him.

'The weather has been unusually warm for this time of year,' Amanda said.

'Huh, if you think this is warm, you'd think Jamaica was a furnace,' Eugene answered.

'What did you think of Britain when you first arrived?' Amanda directed her question to Eugene.

'The first thing to hit me was the cold. The food was bland. No spices to help with the cold weather.'

'I can imagine. What on earth made you come yere from a sunny country like Jamaica?'

'We were lured here. Hopeful of a bright future. The prospect was dangled before us of fantastic self-improvement. Magazines opened a world before the readers eyes. A world bounded only by the readers imagination. We were innocent of the reality of rain and poverty. These adverts tapped into our idealisms. They told us we were bound to succeed if we worked hard,' Eugene stopped to put a piece of food from a fork into his mouth. He chewed slowly for a few seconds before continuing.

'We had British fever. It was the timeshare of those days. We were eager to be a part of this great experiment. A cruel hoax, which we fell for. We were so stupid. We should have realised. The British Empire was an abomination. Founded on slavery.'

'Not at the dinner table,' Hortense's voice was stern and serious.

'If the girl wants to know.'

Amanda felt her ears turning red. 'I'm sorry,' she said quietly.

'No don't you be sorry. You have nothing to be sorry for,' Eugene resumed. 'People should know. Four hundred and ninety-two of us arrived that day.' The others continued eating, seeming uninterested in the conversation, eyes kept on the plates in front of them. 'Dazed and travel stained. We stared in confusion. We were expecting a land of green fields and pretty sleepy villages. Instead, there were grey skies, and when we got to London, oh my. A city of bleak buildings, smog and drizzle. So, this was to be the land of milk and honey we thought.' His voice became more musing, 'I see the pictures now. Embarking off that ship with wide grins. Reminiscent of service men, off to fight for their country against German tyranny. Confident they would win the war. Unbeknown to them, they would return victorious but shell-shocked. Yes, we came here for a better life,' his voice had suddenly taken on an acidic tone, 'and were treated like dogs. So of course, we fought back like dogs.'

'American soldiers, were just as bad, and they were not all white,' Shanice said, 'GI brides.'

Amanda looked at her curiously.

'They told British women how wonderful America was,' Shanice explained. 'The way America was depicted in films at the time didn't help. All sophistication, big houses and cars. The women married them and went to America, only to find they were living in the swamps of the Deep South. Rickety wooden houses, with no electricity or running water.'

'That's women for you,' Desmond grinned.

'We came to Casteldaeg,' Eugene took up his previous conversation, 'as all races had been living here for years. Yemenis, Somalis, Arabians, sailors. We were wanted here, to work at the steelworks and docks.'

'A lot of mixed bloods,' Shanice said. 'We're thoroughbreds.'

'Do you want anything else,' Desmond asked Amanda, who like everyone else, had stopped eating. 'Any more tea.'

'No, I'm fine thanks. That was delicious.'

'Come on then, I'll show you around the area,' Desmond stood up.

'Do you need a hand with the washing up?' Amanda looked at the mess of plates on the table. Charred remains of rejected parts of jerk chicken and limp lettuce.

'No, no, you just be on your way,' Hortense flapped her hands at them.

'Thank you so much Mrs Brown. That was a wonderful meal.'

'Not at all. And less of this Mrs Brown. Call me Hortense.'

Amanda and Desmond left the house, and walked along the terraced streets, which exuded the same spicy scents. Amanda was fascinated by the shops they passed. There was a building with minarets and cupolas, which took her back to the colourful pictures in a book about Ali Baba, which many children took from the book cupboard at school, and pored over the exotic illustrations with fascination. Some buildings had murals on the sides of the walls.

'Maybe I should 'ave brought some presents for the kids,' Amanda said.

'Nah,' Desmond dismissed, 'they get enough as it is.'

'Well, at least a bottle of wine for your parents. I just didn't think.'

'Don't worry about it, we're not really wine drinkers. Mum tries to avoid it at the dinner table. Doesn't want to encourage dad. Guinness and condensed milk. Now there's a nice drink for you.'

'Urgh, I couldn't think of anything worse. I don't like Guinness at the best of times, let alone with thick, syrupy condensed milk.'

'Hey Des, how's it going my man?' a man in his twenties, black, a bit shorter than Desmond, with Rastafarian plaits resting on his shoulders, held his palm high and open as he approached Desmond. Desmond did the same, palms smacking noisily together.

'Hey Leroy, how's it going Bro?'

'Fine with me. I'm going to meet Sammy and Co at the wine bar.'

'Yeah. You look dressed for a glass of wine, too.' Leroy wore a track suit jacket, over a tee shirt and black jeans.

'What you mean? This is smart.'

'For you maybe.'

'Aw, we won't be staying there. Down the Behwearf afterwards. Where you off then?'

'This is Amanda. I'm showing her around the place.'

'Yeah, welcome to the suburbs Amanda,' he held out his hand, with a beaming grin.

'Are you still working at the bakery?' Desmond enquired.

'Yeah, and it's killing me man. I have to get up so early.'

'Hang on in there, at least you get free cakes.'

'Yeah, the old girl, Stacey and the kids love it. I've never known them so pleased to come and visit Uncle Leroy.'

'I bet.'

'Will you be popping into the Behwearf later?'

'Doubt it, better things to do.'

'Take her to the Behwearf, somewhere good, don't bore her to death with some boring pub.'

'Well I won't be taking her to the Duke, that's for sure. Anyway, best get going, you don't want to miss your wine.'

'See you around. Nice meeting you Amanda. Hope to see you at the Behwearf some time.'

'He seems a good laugh,' Amanda said as they continued their walk.

'He's alright. OK Mo,' Desmond acknowledged a man passing, who seemed to be of Indian descent.

Desmond pointed out places with pride, as if he had designed them himself. How happy and animated he was, encountering people he knew on the streets. Amanda appreciated how different Casteldaeg was to Aedre.

'That was Neville,' Desmond said about a young black man he had just waved to, on the other side of the road. 'His father was a clever man. Wanted to be a doctor. Applied to medical school, but was refused. So stupid, a great loss to society, especially when doctors are in such demand. He could have saved lives, but became a taxi driver. Has suffered with depression most of his life.'

'I'm not surprised.'

'These houses were built for the sea workers,' Desmond explained, and pointed out grander houses, which were once owned by merchants and captains. They came to a gathering of what appeared to be municipal houses.

'I don't know if I want to go in there,' Amanda said warily.

'Why not!'

'It looks a bit rough to me.'

'It's not that bad honestly. You won't get ambushed by bandits.'

Amanda walked tentatively, keeping her eyes on all the corners. They passed shops selling produce Amanda had never seen, apart from on documentary programmes. Mangos, plantains and funny looking potatoes. They emerged from the housing cluster, to an area of trendy looking apartment blocks, bars and restaurants, alongside an expanse of sea. Amanda's shoulders relaxed and she gave out a long, audible out breath. There was an aroma of garlic and charred meats.

'What a difference,' Amanda gazed at the bars and restaurants they passed.

'Yeah, this area used to be all houses and warehouses. They were all pulled down. Slum clearance it was called. They wanted to get us out of the way. Not to spoil their stylish city. The power of market forces. Opportunistic destruction. They wouldn't do it in places like Cambridge, where there is a conservation order on every stone.'

'You sound like Wayne now.'

They walked for another fifteen minutes, and they were back at Desmond's house. The children had left, his parents were watching television, and his sister was back reading her magazines. Bailey came over to greet them, and Amanda stroked his head.

'We're going to listen to records in my room for a while,' Desmond said from the opened door of the lounge.

'There's still some carrot cake left,' said Hortense.

'Oh, no thanks Hortense. I couldn't eat another thing, as delicious as it was,' Amanda patted her stomach.

Desmond closed the door and led the way upstairs. Amanda noticed how tidy his room was. A not large, square room, scented with the smell of spices from the evening meal. The walls were painted a mild green, and the duvet cover was dark green, with mint green pillow cases. A poster of the Jamaican flag decorated one wall. There was a wardrobe and two chests of drawers, all of dark wood. There were three short shelves, two of which were filled with books, some on football, and one with photographs of Jamaica. The remaining shelf was a row of CDs, from which Desmond took one. At the end of one shelf was a toy plane, and the other a carving of a tortoise.

'*Songs in the Key of Life* by Stevie Wonder is nice,' Desmond said. 'Do you want to sit on the floor?' he pointed to two cushions next to the window sill.

'Where did you get that tortoise from?' Amanda pointed to the carving on the shelf.

'That's not a tortoise,' Desmond's voice was slightly sardonic, but with humour, 'it's a turtle. I made it in school.'

He passed the wooden carving to her.

'It's lovely,' she said, turning it over in her hands. The shell was painted aqua marine, and the body green.

'Give over,' Desmond chortled, 'it's wonky, not all the legs are the same size.'

'Well it's better than anything I could make,'

'I don't think carpentry was my talent.'

Desmond sat beside Amanda, one leg bent, the other stretched out in front of him, one arm around Amanda's shoulders.

'So how did you find my side of Casteldaeg?' Desmond asked softly.

'Wonderful. Your family are so lush. The food was fantastic. I've never tasted anything like it.'

'Better than an Indian takeaway?' Desmond grinned.

'One 'undred times better. Wayne can remember the first one in the village. The Taj Mahal it was called.'

'They were all called that then. Either that, or the New Delhi.'

'The apprentices all went there, after they had finished their college course. An Indian waiter asked them 'ow they wanted their curries. Mild, medium, 'ot, very 'ot or vindaloo. One of them said, "I'll 'ave a vindaloo."'

'Ridiculous,' Desmond chortled.

'Do you think he could eat it?' Amanda put on an expression of disbelief. 'He must 'ave drunk about a gallon of water.'

'That would have made his mouth cold, making the curry even hotter. I bet the kitchen staff were killing themselves laughing. I see it now, when we've gone to an Indian after a night out, some drunkards call the waiter, "Hey Ahmed," Desmond clicked his fingers. 'Ahmed isn't even an Indian name, it's Arabic. "What's is the hottest thing on the menu," Desmond mouthed. 'They must think it is an act of bravado'

They stopped talking. A melodious track was playing. Amanda lay her head on Desmond's shoulder. She thought how her life had changed so dramatically in the past two weeks. A few weeks ago, her life had consisted of working in the salon. The Futures on a Friday night and the Rugby on a Saturday. Going no further than the villages, apart from the odd shopping trip to Casteldaeg. The rugby club she thought. Four brick walls and a red light. Now here she was, in a part of Casteldaeg, few in Aedre knew existed. Yet here she was, next to this gorgeous, exciting man. Almost intuitively, Desmond turned towards her. They looked at each other wordlessly for a few seconds, and for a moment, she lived in those dark brown orbs of his eyes. He tilted slowly towards her and put his mouth on hers. Ever so gently, but for Amanda it was like a shot of electricity, switching on a neon light. The delirium of the kiss continued for some time, until the CD ended.

'It's time I introduced you to Bob Marley,' Desmond levered himself from the floor by one arm, and changed the disc. The reverberating pulse of a reggae beat filled the room.

'He was only thirty-six when he died, wasn't he?' Amanda asked.

'Bob Marley never died,' Desmond said with mock derision. 'A man like that. He lives on. His music, his words, his inspiration.' Desmond became lost in thought. 'He was born in the ghettos of Jamaica, where violence was glorified. There seemed to be no way out, but he did though. Just shows what can be done, he fought his way out, and fought all his life. Against oppression.' Desmond stared contemplatively at the opposite wall. 'He gave a free concert, in the hope of easing tension between political parties. Someone attempted to assassinate him. He and his wife were injured.'

'So much for easing of tension.'

'He had a spider named after him.'

'Ger out,' Amanda laughed.

'No seriously, he had an underwater spider named after him, Desis bobmarleyi.'

'Spiders don't live underwater. You're 'aving me on.'

'It's true. You look it up.'

'I don't know if I would want a spider to be named after me. I don't like them. I was at my friend Laura's 'ouse once, and this massive spider walked across the floor. Well, we couldn't do a thing. We both had our legs up on the chair, and Laura was pointing at it going "Get lost, get lost."'

'Laura, which friend is that?'

'Oh, I 'aven't seen her for a long time. She went to Italy to work as a nanny. She met this guy, Giuseppe. She gave 'im my number once, and said if he rings tell 'im this, and said something in Italian. I said "ang on", I wrote it down. Good job he didn't ring, otherwise I would 'ave been El...l... l... l...Fandango.'

'El Fandango,' Desmond laughed. 'I'm sure she didn't say that. Did you ever think of going to Italy to see her?'

'No, I went to Spain about a year ago, with Sharon and two others. There was these German boys staying in the 'otel. One night they came back singing on top of their voices down the corridor, must 'ave been about one o'clock in the morning. "DEUTCHLAND, AUSCHWITZ, BA BOOM BA BOOM."'

'I doubt they were singing Auschwitz,' Desmond laughed with slight derision.

'That's what it sounded like.'

'Anyway,' Desmond checked his watch, 'it's time we should go, I don't want your family thinking I've kidnapped you.'

I wish you would Amanda thought, but reluctantly stood up, and patted down her clothes. She again thanked Hortense, Eugene and Shanice before she left. Hortense gave her a bear hug, and Eugene shook her hand.

'It's been a pleasure,' Eugene said, his breath exuded a faded smell of rum.

Bailey accompanied them to the door, for a last pat before they left.

Chapter 5

Amanda walked through the side streets with her friend Sharon. Sharon was talking fervently about how she was looking forward to the evening without her boyfriend Robert. It was Saturday night, and they were making their way to the Futures. Amanda noticed how monochrome the streets looked. Yet they sparkled with life when she was with Desmond. They reached the Futures and pushed their way through a fog of nicotine and a forest of boring polo shirts, to find a patch of space in the lounge.

'I'll get the first-round in. What are you 'aving?' Sharon asked.

'The usual. 'Arf lager.'

Amanda looked around the room uninterestedly. She looked over the heads of youths, with their fingers wrapped around pint or half pint glasses brimming with amber liquid, at the red, flock wall paper. She thought of Desmond, and how he seemed to draw everyone in the room towards him. His smile was like a lighthouse. Now and again a screech of female laughter would pierce the drone of chattering voices. There was the yeasty smell of beer and nicotine. She picked out Bobo in the crowd. His face marred from battles with acne. There was Donald, so pudgy, his face seemed to be without bones.

'Well, you look like you've lost 'alf a crown and found sixpence,' Sharon returned with the drinks.

'Yeah, well, it's 'ardly the most exciting of places is it?'

'Best that's around unfortunately. So, you're not with Desmond tonight then?' It was put more as a question than a statement.

'Wish I was.'

'Thanks'

'No, I don't mean it like that,' Amanda said quickly. 'Oh, I don't know. You know what I mean. You only see guys like 'im in magazines,' she said dreamily.

'Well, no offence, but personally, I've seen better. Keanu Reeves for instance. Now you're talking,' Sharon's eyes brightened.

'Doesn't look much like Robert.'

'You can say that again,' Sharon said scathingly. 'Mind you, *he* can make my heart race.' Sharon nodded towards a young man of about six foot, with short dark hair. He was draped decoratively over the bar, dressed in jeans, and a short brown bomber jacket.

'Awright both,' a skinny boy appeared. He was about eighteen. Black hair, short on the sides, yet thick on top. He was wearing faded jeans, which were clumped around his waist by a tightened belt. A black short sleeved polo shirt revealed punctured forearms.

'Awright Scoobs,' Sharon answered, and Amanda smiled. 'Not drunk yet then are you?'

'Not yet, but I'm getting there. Anyway, there's a rave going on in Coopers field tonight. Are you going?'

'How about it?' Sharon asked Amanda eagerly.

'Aw, I don't know,' Amanda said hesitatingly.

'Aw come on. It'll be a laugh,' Sharon enthused.

'It'll be good,' said the skinny boy, 'Axel's bringing a generator, and he knows some people with great equipment.'

'We're going to the rugby club,' Amanda said.

'How boring is that,' said the boy ''ave some real action.'

'I'll think about it,' Amanda replied.

'Yeah, so I may see you there then,' the boy disappeared into the throng.

'Come on,' Sharon persuaded, 'you were only saying earlier, how boring this place is. Let's try something different to the rugby club.'

'Yeah, but raves,' Amanda said dubiously, 'all those drugs, it's not my scene.'

'You don't 'ave to take drugs. I don't. Not everyone there is taking them. There's probably people around you now who've taken something tonight.'

'My father won't be 'appy, with me going there.'

'Don't tell 'im. Try it anyway, and if you don't like it, you can always leave. Nothing is going to 'appen to you there. People just go there to dance and 'ave a good time. What else are you going to do? Mope around yere and go home miserable?' Sharon said reprovingly.

'Ok then, we better get some drinks in us, to get into the party mood.'

'That's the way,' Sharon smiled with satisfaction.

Alcohol had turned Amanda's reticence into excited anticipation, as she made her way with Sharon through overhangs of leaves and small branches to Coopers field. They tried to keep their eyes on others a few yards ahead, but were kept back by laughing, every time one of them stumbled, or said something which they would not normally find amusing, but at this moment was hilarious.

'We don't want to lose them,' Amanda giggled, 'the last place we want to get stuck is out yere.'

'Don't worry, there'll be plenty of others close behind. Besides, we'll just follow the music. Look, yere comes Beezer. You're off to the rave then are you?'

'Aye, looking for a woman.'

'You're 'oping, aren't you?'

'Anyone can pull at a rave.'

'Hate to tell you this Buddy, but people go to a rave to dance these days. You're in the wrong times.'

'We'll see,' he and another three boys went past Amanda and Sharon, and were soon ahead of them.

The music got louder and louder, and they saw strobe lights stroke the sky, like radar seeking aircraft. The lights illuminated the bobbing heads of a large crowd.

'Crickey!' said Amanda, 'I 'aven't seen as many people as this since we went to that festival in Casteldaeg park.'

'Do you want some water, girls?' a young man handed them each a plastic bottle filled with water, which they took. 'If you need a refill, there's a stream over there.'

'You can't drink that,' Amanda laughed.

'Yeah, it's ok,' the young man replied, 'probably better than what comes out of your tap.'

'Is this what this is?' Amanda held up the bottle, peering at the contents.

'Naw, we filled them up in the Future's toilets.'

'Not from the actual toilet I 'ope,' at which point she and Sharon collapsed with laughter.

'The taps,' the young man shook his head slowly.

'Look at Digby over there,' Amanda laughed. 'What's he on?'

Digby approached, on seeing them pointing and laughing at him.

'It's in the trees man. They're so green and perfect, and we're chopping them down. We're messing up the planet man.'

'What 'ave you taken Digs?' Sharon laughed.

'I'm telling you man, I'm gonna see the sun rise tomorrow. What an amazing sight.'

They then glimpsed Melissa draped against a fencepost, talking to a boy in his mid-teens, who seemed to be having difficulty following the conversation.

'Hey girls, great seeing you,' Melissa shouted and walked over to them.

'Are you with 'im?' Sharon nodded towards the boy Melissa had just been talking to.

'No, but I hope to be by two-thirty. Where's the black hottie tonight then?'

'Out with his friends I expect,' Amanda replied evasively.

'Ah,' Melissa drawled, 'so you're foot loose and fancy free tonight then. Looking for some fun?'

'No,' Amanda replied neutrally, 'I've just come to dance.'

'Well, there's a lot of that going on,' Sharon grabbed Amanda's arm, and pulled her into the crowd.

'If you want any E's,' shouted Melissa, 'go see Jay.'

The darkness suddenly exploded with a spectrum of throbbing colours and fizzing music. The crowd had a pulse all of its own. There was a frenzy of strobe lights. A fluorescent alcoholic atmosphere. The beat of the music was hypnotic, inducing a trancelike state. Amanda's body swayed instinctively, and she believed she was dancing amazingly well. She had rhythm, so she thought, as did Desmond. She had seen Desmond dance to a CD in his bedroom, that night she was there, and was mesmerised by his movement. How effortless it seemed for him to move so well. Boys she danced with at the rugby club, danced stiffly. They didn't use their hips like Desmond. Their dancing seemed a form of walking on the spot. She thought of Nigel, and how awkward he seemed when dancing. Self-conscious, as if he shouldn't be doing it. She looked at those around her. At all the people dancing and flailing their arms around. Every so often they would all raise their hands in the air in unison. She and Sharon would join them, and Amanda felt a connection with the crowd.

She was immersed in a wall of smoke, strobes and electronic music, and felt a spreading sensation in her chest. A euphoric rush of energy was fizzing in her body, swirling sensations, turning her body into a sleek, speedy sports car. She looked up into the sky, which was sparkling with stars, like a glass of bubbling champagne. The navy black sky was swarming with tiny silver points. The moon dripped light over the mountains, and onto the rooftops of the village below. She had a feeling of connection with something bigger. She felt liberated, and looked at those around her, who all seemed to be feeling the same. Most were dressed in jeans and tee shirts. Some had bandanas around their foreheads. This was better than any nightclub, Amanda thought. No stuffy dress codes. Clothes are just material she now realised. How meaningless and superficial, all this dressing up to go to night clubs, on the rare occasions she managed to go to one. This is what matters, she thought, the here and now, and we all know it. Amanda was still feeling exhilarated when the music stopped, and the crowd were dispersing.

'Where are they going?' Amanda was still dancing, arms flailing about, 'Why 'as the music stopped?'

'Come on you nutter,' Sharon grabbed her arm and was pulling her.

'I'm not going 'ome this time of night,' Amanda shouted defiantly, her pulse was still kicking furiously.

'It's four o'clock in the morning!'

They staggered out of the field, making their way over glinting crushed cans, which were strewn across trampled grass. They were laughing clouds of white breath, and were soggy with perspiration. The night was beginning to sink warmly between the mountains, and soon dawn would be alighting on the tarmac and brick of the villages. Amanda felt she was walking on springs.

'What a night,' Sharon remarked jubilantly, 'I bet you're glad you came now.'

'You bet, imagine missing that. Life can never be the same after that. And that was YERE, IN AEDRE!'

They walked buoyantly down the mountain. The first layers of light were breaking over the horizon.

'Stop!' Amanda grabbed Sharon's arm and went rigid.

'What's the matter?' Sharon said with concern.

'Look 'ow beautiful it is,' Amanda stared at the village below.

'Aven't you ever seen Aedre this time of the morning?'

'Ow quiet, 'ow green the mountains are, the trees.'

'You sound like Digby now. It's quiet because everyone is in bed. Where I wanna be, so come on.'

They continued walking, over grass glistening with dew, accompanied by birdsong, until they reached the village.

'What are you up to tomorrow then,' Amanda asked

'Tomorrow!'

'Well today really.'

'I dunno, and won't be able to make a decision until I get some sleep. How 'bout you?'

'Get some sleep, dinner, then over to Rosaline's.'

Yeah, ok, bye then.'

'Bye'

They parted to walk different ways. Amanda noticed a chill around her, so she tucked her blouse, which she had perspired through, into her jeans. Should have brought a jacket or jumper she shivered, but I didn't expect to be out until this time. Mam and Dad are not going to be pleased with me. In fact, Dad is going to have an ep. She ran her trailing fingers alongside the iron railings of the park. The rising sun lay stripes of light over the pavement. She stopped at the top of the railway bridge.

'I am the salmon in the sandwiches,' she shouted to the empty space around her.

'I am the tuna in the tin;

I am the cold cola waiting to be poured from the can;

I am the unwrapped birthday present.'

She continued shouting, as she staggered along and reached her street.

'I am the song everyone sings;

I AM IN LOVE.'

'Bloody shurrup down there,' someone shouted from an upstairs window, 'five o'clock in the bloody morning.'

'Free country innit,' Amanda shouted back, whilst fumbling around with her key.

'I'll bloody free country you, if I come down there. I'll free country you around the ear 'ole. Now move or I'll call the police.'

'I can't get my key in the door.'

'It's not your bloody door that's why,' the window was slammed shut.

Chapter 6

Amanda lay under the duvet for those few moments between sleeping and waking, when she didn't know why or where she was. The insistent siren of a fire engine from the outside world, brought knowledge of her existence slowly seeping into her brain. She pulled the covers tightly around her, and tried to sink back into the corridors of sleep. It was of no use, the sound of pots and pans landing on surfaces, her father's argumentative voice, and her brothers bantering retorts drifted up the stairs. Amanda groaned, lay on her back, and watched some flies dancing around the ceiling above her. Watching them move in a figure of eight formation. She looked at the clock radio on the small cabinet beside her. The clock flashed nine-thirty, and she knew she could not remain in the cocoon of the duvet any longer.

Grudgingly she pulled back the covers, and her feet tentatively found the softness of carpet. A thin, weak streak of light stretched across the carpet. She lumbered over to the window and grabbed the sides of the curtains. She felt the soft, cat's tongue roughness of the velvet, and let out another groan, on pulling the curtains apart, when light came crashing through. Gradually, her eyes focussed on the back garden. Samson was sitting on his stomach, watching birds from the path. His fur gleamed pale orange. Tail moved back and forth like a metronome, knowing from experience, it was pointless to chase. She swallowed a sigh and moved to the wardrobe. There was a malty warmth in the room. The weak aroma of perfume floated out of the wardrobe when she opened the doors. Remnants of the previous evening clinging to her clothes. She grabbed her blouse. That should have been put in the wash basket she thought. Before leaving the room, she turned to look at the bed she would make, after a shower. The pillow still held the shape of her head.

'You've decided to get up then?' Gerald said, when Amanda emerged into the lounge, after she had eased her way down the stairs, her face washed and teeth cleaned. Gerald's face was set in a grim scowl.

Amanda was wearing a long white shirt over a pair of denim shorts. She carried a mug of steaming powdered coffee. There was the smell of roasting meat juices pervading the room. The sound of the radio and Mair's singing emanated from the kitchen.

'She looks well considering how much she drank last night,' Wayne chirped from the sofa.

'She 'as Aedre immunity,' Neil chipped in.

'Ow do you know 'ow much I 'ad to drink,' Amanda's voice was surly, whilst she scuffed patterns in the carpet with her big toe.

'I heard you out in the street. Woke me up at five this morning,' said Wayne

'WHAT TIME?!' Gerald bellowed. 'You've gone all to pot since spending time with that Jamaican. People like 'im always spell trouble.'

'What do you mean people like 'im?' Amanda sat upright and glared.

'Rastafarian. That lot with their drugs and plaits,' Gerald practically spat. 'They come over yere with their loads of children, and expect the state to pay for them. It's a bloody disgrace.'

'Here's the hangover sauce,' Wayne reappeared from the kitchen, and placed a bacon sandwich next to her coffee which had now gone cold.

'Desmond and his family aren't claiming benefits,' Amanda said indignantly, eyes bulging. 'They 'ave worked all their lives. He 'asn't got plaits, and he doesn't take drugs. They don't follow that culture. Desmond just wants respect and peace.'

'I'll give them respect and bloody peace,' Gerald admonished. 'I'd cut their plaits and benefits and send them back to where they came from. Then Britain can 'ave some *peace*. Bloody scrounging sods.'

'Where are you going to send them back to?' Wayne interjected. 'Many of them were born here.'

'A lot of them wouldn't 'ave come yere, 'ad they known what they were to face,' Amanda said angrily. 'American imperialists, who dragged them out of Africa in the first place and treated them like chattels.'

'Wasn't all Westerners,' said Wayne, 'some Africans were just as complicit in the slave trade.'

'Since when did you become an expert on American history?' Gerald looked at Amanda with scorn. 'You've been brainwashed by jungle man.'

'Oh yeah,' Amanda objected, 'so we're cleaner, healthier and safer now, but are we any 'appier? Especially when people condemn on the basis of colour. You keep telling me of the times you were all black. All covered in coal dust.'

'The difference is, he can't wash his colour off,' Gerald shouted.

'You think it's all mud huts and big chiefs in Jamaica. Well it's not. There are people there living in luxury, in gated communities, with servants.'

'Yeah, they need to be gated an' all, for protection. If Jamaica is so bloody wonderful, why don't they all go back there?'

'Ok, that's enough for a Sunday morning,' Wayne placated. 'And here's Anita,' he said at the sound of the doorbell.

'Morning everyone,' Anita breezed into the lounge. 'Well, still just about morning. Morning Mair,' she shouted to the kitchen. 'What's happened here then, war been declared or something?'

'You could say that,' Neil muttered.

'Yeah, let's get some cheer in yere,' Amanda switched on the television to a music station.

'Not that station again,' Gerald moaned, 'in my day we only 'ad *Top of the Pops* and *Jukebox Jury*. Now it's on all bloody day, and all the music sounds the same. No wonder the kids are like they are. I see them going about with 'oles in their jeans.'

'Grunge,' Neil laughed, 'Youth protest.'

'Aye, yes, that's nothing new. In my day, it was flower power. Hippies thinking they had the revelatory drug with marijuana. I see them now, as plumbers and teachers.'

'I can't imagine you Gerry, with long hair and a spliff,' Anita said with humour.

'I didn't 'ave anything to do with it. A pint down the Drag, a game of darts, that's all I needed.'

'Good old steady Gerry,' Anita grinned.

'And he brought up three beautiful children,' said Neil.

'I see there's been another attack on an 'oliday cottage in North Wales,' Gerald went back to his newspaper. 'Another nationalist arsonist. Bloody stupid. The place would 'ave decayed had it not been bought for an 'oliday 'ome.'

'I'm laying the table,' Mair went from the kitchen to the dining room.

'I'll help you,' Anita jumped up from the sofa between Wayne and Amanda.

Soon they were all seated around the table, passing around dishes heaped with vegetables, and a plate laden with slices of meat.

Dinner was fraught however, Amanda was monosyllabic.

'Where did you go last night?' Anita enquired of Amanda.

'Oh, don't ask,' said Wayne.

'Out until five this morning,' Gerald said grudgingly.

'Ah, a good night then,' said Anita.

'I don't know what's 'appened to her, since she's been seeing that Desmond,' Mair joined in. 'And what's all this I'm 'earing from Don, about you giving 'im cheek the other night at his club.'

'He refused to serve Desmond,' Amanda said sullenly, 'and some old men were going on about 'ow they fought to save the country from the likes of 'im.'

'And so they did,' Gerald said tetchily.

'Oh for goodness sake,' Anita said frustratedly, 'they fought against a fascist dictator, who believed Germany to be the superior race. They were fighting against racism, not for it.'

Mair went into the kitchen, and returned with an enormous apple pie and a dish of moulded yellow cream.

'Problem is,' Neil said, 'there's never been any black people in the villages. There was Kai Lu Chen, who joined my school when he was ten. Everyone assumed he was Chinese. His parents opened the first Chinese take away, but he was probably Vietnamese.'

'This is all your fault,' Mair directed her vitriol at Neil. 'What did you want to bring 'im back yere for?'

'Oh come on,' Wayne remonstrated, 'he's alright. He's not a gangster. He seems a nice bloke to me.'

'Milk and tar never mix,' Gerald said glumly. 'Their ways are not like ours. Look what 'appened in India when we left it. Hindus and Muslims tearing each other apart. They are uncivilised. We tried to give them law and respect, and what did they do?'

'We went in there and plundered the country,' Anita said accusingly, 'tried to impose our ways, then left when we could no longer afford to do so. Left them with nothing.'

'Let's not get into politics over dinner please,' Neil pleaded.

Chapter 7

'What an epic night we 'ad last night,' Amanda said across the table from Rosaline, and took another sip from her coffee. Light through the slats of vertical blinds, had cast a Jacobs Ladder on the opposite wall. She had so badly wanted to share her excitement from the previous evening with Rosaline. Her enthusiasm however, had gradually dampened throughout the day. 'We were hanging though.'

'They'll be stopping all that soon,' Rosaline's older sister Janet entered the kitchen. Janet was tall and slim with dyed blonde hair. Small age lines were appearing at the corners of her eyes.

'Why? we were harming nobody. We were out of the way,'

'Dear, dear me. People having fun in Aedre, we can't 'ave that,' Janet shook her head in mock disparagement. 'You know what people are like around yere. Complaints are being made about youths rampaging through the streets in the early hours of the morning.'

'Best we 'ave something like that. Stops kids vandalising,' Amanda said defensively.

'The Emerald, now there was a pub for you,' Janet who had taken a chair at the table with them, took a cigarette to her lips and sucked in some smoke. Her face was dreamy with reminiscence. 'The Emerald was a base for visionaries, squares, all sorts went there.'

'The Emerald!' both Amanda and Rosaline could not keep the laughter out of their voices. 'That spit and sawdust place?' said Amanda.

'Never used to be like that,' Janet said peevishly. 'Everybody used to go there. Well, anybody who was anybody. If you wanted to see someone who was worth seeing, you'd go to the Emerald on a Friday night. I wouldn't go there now though. Not with clean shoes anyway.'

'Don't need to now, do you,' Amanda said, ''appily married woman. You 'ave everything you want in Mal.'

'Talking of 'im, I best get going, otherwise he will be wondering where I am. That's marriage for you.'

'Did you meet 'im at the Emerald?' Amanda asked.

'Naw, it was the Old Grey. He was with Juice.'

'I bet Juice was pissed, was he?'

'Now is the Pope Catholic?' Janet said derisively. 'The whole two years I was going with Mal, I only saw Juice sober once, and that was on the morning of our wedding.'

'Is he still like that?'

'Can't afford to be now can he? Married with a kid, and another one on the way. They don't even go to the rugby on match days any longer. Towser has a super-duper large screen TV, so they go and watch them at his place. Get some cans from the Co-op.'

'Times 'ave changed,' said Amanda.

'You can say that again, and the charts ain't what they used to be. How can a song like "Pump Up the Volume, Pump Up the Volume," Janet sang in a deep voice, 'get to number one?!'

'New Romantic wasn't much better,' said Amanda, 'all electronic.'

'I preferred the seventies, I liked Soul. Anyway, nice to see you Amanda, I'll be around on Tuesday afternoon Ros. Bye both.'

'My goodness,' Amanda said as soon as Janet had left, 'I thought any minute she was going to come out with Perry Como.'

'No taste, see.'

'Little 'appened around yere until Des came along.'

'Was that until last night?'

'Yeah, but I was wishing Des was there all the time. I wanted 'im to see 'ow good it was.'

'Ello Amanda, 'ow are you?' Rosaline's mother Agnes enquired. Agnes always appeared tired to Amanda, behind her make up, and her hands were always chapped.

'Oh, I'm Ok Mrs Evans. 'Ow are you?'

'Oh, plodding along see. Look at that pile of junk out there now,' Agnes pointed to a rusting Datsun on the neighbours drive. 'I 'ave to look at that every day.'

'What's he 'oping to do with it?' Amanda's features creased into puzzlement.

'Goodness knows. Been there too long if you ask me. 'Ow is the family keeping?'

'Oh, fine thanks.'

''Ave you seen Derek Matthews at all?'

'Apart from 'im shouting out his window at me this morning, no.'

'Funny old so and so, Derek.'

Agnes replaced a tea towel then left the kitchen.

'June and Steve were arguing again last night,' Rosaline took up the theme of the Datsun owning neighbours from Agnes.

'Oh, what was it over this time.'

'Goodness knows, I didn't see much of them last week to be fair. I 'ear them shouting to the dogs at night. "Brandy, Whisky,"' Rosaline's voice increased an octave, in mocking imitation of June, '"Shurrup", then you can hear Ben, a childish voice, "Bandy, Whicky, shurrup."'

Amanda was only listening with half her mind however, the other half being on Desmond.

''Ave another cake,' Rosaline pointed to a plate of small cakes in the centre of the table. Amanda declined as she had already eaten two. Rosaline was bigger than Amanda, but did not seem to be perturbed by it. 'Big Ben is 'eavier than me,' she would say. Rosaline worked at a local supermarket, where she stocked shelves and served at the checkout.

'So, you were saying about Des.'

Amanda's eyes lit up. 'My whole life has changed since I met 'im.'

'How does Tiggy feel about that?' Rosaline asked, using the nickname some had for Nigel.

'What's it to do with 'im?!' Amanda looked baffled.

'Well, you 'ave known each other since childhood.'

'So what? I've known you since childhood.'

'You know what I mean. The amount of people who think you and 'e are an item.'

Amanda gave a contrived laugh and shook her head. She thought of Nigel with his dark brown hair, and antifreeze blue eyes. 'What are people like? Nigel and me 'ave been mates for years. I can't imagine anything else. We're more like brother and sister. What is it that people find so difficult understanding that males and females can just be friends? Even Desmond thinks Nigel fancies me.'

'Well, maybe 'e does.'

'Oh, for goodness' sake Rosaline, not you as well,' Amanda looked out the kitchen window.

'Ok, ok,' Rosaline held up her palms in submission. 'I get it. Now tell me about Des.'

'He's so different to the boys around yere Ros.'

'E's 'ardly a boy.'

'Exactly, last week as I was walking 'ome from work, he was waiting on the corner of Thomas St. I wasn't expecting to see 'im, and oh, I looked a mess.'

'I can't imagine you looking a mess.'

'Oh, I was. It had been a busy day. I was dishevelled and greasy with perspiration, but he looked at me as if I was wearing satin and diamonds.'

'What does 'e think of this place then?'

'Oh. He loves it. He could spend all day walking the mountains. Aedre was an unplace to 'im before he came to work yere. Remote and distant. When he told his family he was coming yere to work, his brother said "WHAT, they eat their young up there."'

'Charming,' Rosaline shook her head, 'Ave you met 'im.'

'No, I've met one of his sisters though. She's alright. They're all alright. His mother is lovely, and the food she makes is fabulous.'

'Like what, rhinoceros curry?'

'Give over you. All these different vegetables. Plantain.'

'Plant what?'

'It's like bananas, only they use them like potatoes. You won't get them down the Co-op. They've got a dog.'

'What kind.'

'A Frankenstein dog.'

'What do you mean?'

'I wish I knew. All different bits of dog. Legs of a terrier, head of a Staffy, and a body of an I don't know what. When he barks, he throws his 'ead back, as if needing all his strength to do so. He's nice though. And I've learnt so much since being with Des. He's lent me some Bob Marley CDs. I listen to them constantly on my portable.'

'Bob Marley! He was some African druggie wasn't he?'

'He was Jamaican, and he did smoke the wacky weed, but he wrote brilliant songs. He wanted to change things see. Make the world a better place. He sang about injustice and oppression. "Get on, fight on," Amanda sang, "fight on for your rights." He was only thirty-six when he died. "No Woman, No Cry" is so sad. I cry whenever I 'ear it. He wrote it to reassure his wife, when he was dying from cancer. You can borrow them if you want.'

'No thanks, I think I'll give that one a miss.'

'He was looking through the books on my shelves the other day, and he picked up one of my Ladybird books.'

'Bob Marley?'

'Give over you. One on Romans. I loved the pictures in that one I said. He just laughed, "look 'ow white they are," he said. "The Romans were not just Italians, they also 'ad Moors." Moors were from Africa. He 'ad Aesop's Fables when he was a kid. There was one called the "Lion in love." "There is nothing more dangerous to peace, than the ill-assorted marriage into which reckless love can lead," he said, and gave one of those laughs, which although he had said something serious, it was meant to be funny.'

'Sounds a bit intelligent to me, and you *remembered* it!'

Amanda took a sip of her coffee, which was now over an hour cold.

'I'll 'ave to take you to the Lionstone I said. I did point it out to 'im, from the road, the other day. And I saw it as it really was. A concrete slab laid on top of another concrete slab. "Ardly a fitting burial ground for lions," he said. But it looked so majestic to us when we were kids.'

'Yeah, surprising what an old mining relic can become. We never questioned where the lions came from. Did we actually think lions once roamed Aedre?'

'My parents aren't 'appy about me and Desmond though. "You'll be 'aving coffee-coloured kids if you're not careful," my dad said the other day. Des is far better than those yobs who call 'im things.'

'We never saw colour when we were kids,' Rosaline said matter-of-factly, 'so where did it come from?'

'I don't know,' Amanda said resignedly, and glimpsed at the clock on the wall. 'On that note, I'd better get going.'

Rosaline stood up and accompanied Amanda to the door.

'When you seeing Des next?'

'I'll see 'im at lunch break tomorrow.'

'*Ohhh*, it is serious. When will we next meet?'

'Don't know, I'll call you.'

Amanda heard the click of the door closing, after saying goodbye.

'Hi June,' she said to a woman pegging out the washing in the neighbouring garden.

'Hi Amanda. What do you think about these pissing wheelie bins from the pissing council then?'

'My mother was moaning about them. Supposed to be easier to move. They're almost as big as my mother.'

'I know. Pissing useless.'

Chapter 8

What a magical morning it is, Amanda thought whilst blurred images rushed past the train window she was gazing through. Aedre was rapidly receding into the distance. Bronze light gilded the rails of the opposite track. She was being treated today. A meal at an Italian restaurant, and the pictures afterwards, but first, Desmond was taking her to the museum. The museum! Imagine that. He was taking her to see some pot that had been excavated on the other side of the Sceard. She hadn't been to the museum since junior school. She had not been impressed from what she could remember. Rooms and rooms of different objects. One full of china cups and saucers, another of rocks and stone crosses. Well supposed to be a cross, but more like a stone stick with a circle on top. Celtic crosses they had been labelled. She remembered Nigel being excited and rushing up to her as they had been gathered to leave. 'Did you go down the mine?' he gushed, eyes sparkling. 'Yeah,' she had nodded, she didn't think it was that good. Some narrow basement room, with shop dummies dressed in dirty overalls and black faces, on their knees with pickaxes in their hands, behind glass panes. But Desmond wanted to take her there, and a warmth spread through her at the thought. She could not imagine any Aedre boy suggesting that for a date, let alone taking her to a restaurant. The pictures maybe, and at a stretch, buying her some popcorn.

She thought of Desmond, and the speed at which they had become intimate with one another. Speaking on the telephone, oh, how she waited for the ring of the telephone, to hear his voice down the line. They had told each other an assortment of personal details. She had even told him of how she had once dreamt of being a beautician to the stars, and the person behind the glamorous looks of celebrities. How they would go on television displaying her work. They met each other for lunch twice a week. He would come to the salon once a week, and on Wednesdays, she would meet him outside the factory. Hortense would put something extra in his lunchbox for her. She thought of Hortense, and of how the smell of coriander and curry always clung to her. Amanda's neighbours followed their accelerating relationship from doorsteps and twitching curtains. Producing their own little soap opera, much to the chagrin of Mair.

The day was bright and warm. The clouds in the blue sky were like popcorn. She returned to her thoughts. She had married Desmond four times that morning, in her alternative life, during her walk to the station. Imagining their life post marriage. Maybe they would move to Jamaica. She could set up a beauty parlour. Money goes a lot further there than in this country Desmond had said, so maybe they could have a nice house on the beach. Nothing large, they wouldn't need anything too big. Amanda pictured herself standing on the wooden veranda outside their front door in the morning, feeling the sea spray on her face, the sting of salt in her nostrils. The walks they would take together at sundown, past gardens filled with tropical flowers, whose names she could not pronounce. She wondered what her father would say if she told him she was planning to move to Jamaica. 'Silly mango picking country,' he would chide, 'you don't want to go out there, otherwise you'll end up picking mangos for the rest of your life.' 'I don't know about mangos,' Wayne would join in. 'Sugar cane maybe.'

She was jolted from her reverie by the opening of the carriage door, and someone stepping from the platform onto the train. She impatiently waited for the train to leave. There were four landmarks on the train journey from Aedre to Casteldaeg, and she had counted two of them, so there were another two to go, before she arrived at the last stop, where Desmond would be waiting to meet her. She liked the concept of Desmond meeting her on the platform. That was romantic, like one of those old black and white films her mother sometimes watched on a Sunday afternoon. There was the former coalmine, one of the landmarks, now dolled up as a museum.

She had made up carefully that morning, as if preparing for a photoshoot, even though Desmond always tried to dissuade her from wearing makeup. 'Why cover such perfect skin?' he would say, 'No,' she would retort, 'You have perfect skin, your sister has perfect skin, I need to work on it, otherwise people will tell me I look ill.' She had put on a white blouse, with a muted blue stripe, and a white jacket. Desmond had told her she looked good in white. Amanda knew this, as it suited her bronzed complexion, which she achieved with makeup, and helped by her brown hair. Then came the sound of steel against steel, as the wheels of the train slowed to a halt at Amanda's destination. She alighted from the train along with many other passengers. The chemicals of the city hit her. A mingle of smoke and fumes, industry at work, the machinery needed to keep the buildings running. The busy noise of a bustling city also filled the air. Tannoid voices, the rumble of approaching and departing trains, passenger footfall and train doors slamming.

The crowd dissipated a little, descending the steps leading from the platform, and there she saw Desmond walking towards her, with his indulgent smile. That smile, which made all the troubles of the world disappear, so they would be in their own private heaven. Her mouth and tongue went slack, as if filled with a sugary syrup. She tasted love on her tongue, and flung her arms around Desmond, brushing her lips against his Paco Rabanne flavoured neck.

'I 'aven't seen you for two days,' she said through quick breaths.

'Well here I am now,' he laughed. He took a step back, holding her hands at arms-length, 'you look beautiful.'

'You're looking great yourself.'

She could see he had made an effort. He was wearing navy blue chinos, with a pale blue shirt. He had a jumper slung over his back. Sleeves tied loosely around his neck. She linked her arm into his, and floated along beside him out of the station, to the traffic-infested street. They crossed at traffic lights to the civilised world of shops, clubs and restaurants. The buildings were tall, the later ones being made up of much glass, which reflected brightness. Today, the sun made them appear to be beacons. Beacons blasting the message one had arrived somewhere worth arriving at. Amanda was proud to be holding onto Desmond's arm. Other pedestrians however, seemed not to notice, and just strode past, faces set in determination, as if focussing on some target. Amanda looked at the large faces of men and women, staring down at them from advertising boards.

'Casteldaeg is such an 'appening place,' she enthused, tightening her grip on Desmond's arm.

'Give me not-happening Aedre any day.'

'Are you mad?!'

'Take the mountains, the views, the quietness, and the freshness of the air. I mean, you can't beat that.'

'You 'ave your parks yere.'

'Yeah, and they're always full of people, the noise and smell of traffic is always nearby.'

'All the nightlife and restaurants you 'ave. The only places I 'ave are the Futures or the Rugby. Take it or leave it.'

The traffic had congealed again, as they reached the outer road which encircled the city. They took the subway to reach the museum. They passed a homeless person huddled at the entrance to the subway, with a small box in front of him. He mumbled 'Spare change,' at each passer-by. Desmond dug the fingers of his free hand into his trouser pocket, and tossed some coins into the box.

'Is that your idea of things happening?' he said wryly.

Amanda shrugged her shoulders uncomfortably, as they emerged from the subway to a wide avenue of lavish, ornate buildings.

'Well, here's the museum,' the enthusiasm had returned to Desmond's voice. He led her along the high-ceilinged corridor to an expansive room, filled with objects encased in glass.

'Here it is,' Desmond proudly pointed to a large pot in a glass case, as if showing her a masterpiece he had painted. Amanda however stared at the pot, but failed to summon any enthusiasm. It just looked like a large rusting pot to her.

'This was found in a lake just over the mountain from you,' he said triumphantly. 'Mountains provided great dips for lakes. Just picture the ghosts of those Neanderthals wandering around the area.' He paused for a moment, 'I wonder if they had any prejudices,' he pondered. 'Well, they weren't Neanderthals who made this. They would have been Iron or Bronze Age, but there must have been Neanderthals there at some point.'

'There's still some there today,' Amanda muttered.

'Is there anything else here you'd like to see?' Desmond said a little deflated.

'Not really.'

'Ok, lunch awaits.'

The air inside the restaurant was blurred with the smell of garlic. The bottom half of the walls were lined with colourful tiles, the top coloured with a wash paint. Pillars were draped with plastic lemons, grapes and garlic, to give some semblance of authenticity to the description of Italian restaurant. Accordion music was being piped through speakers, high on the corners of the walls. The interior was dark, despite the fact it was early afternoon. Once inside, the time of day could not be determined. A waiter led them to a small square table, where red candlewax from a lit candle dripped down over a shiny red check tablecloth.

'This is a right tidy place,' Amanda said, as she took the seat the waiter had pulled from the table for her. 'Ave you been yere before?'

'A few times,' Desmond was reading the menu.

'Yeah, with other girlfriends?'

'Family, special occasions. We came here for my sister's birthday last,' he said nonchalantly.

'What's all this then?' Amanda was looking quizzically at the menu. 'I can't pronounce 'alf of it, Fettuchiny, Rigat......'

'They're all different types of pasta.'

'I think I'll 'ave pizza.'

'That's not very adventurous.'

'Naw, but it's safe.'

'Are you having a starter?'

'I don't want to ruin my appetite.'

'Come on, it's our first restaurant meal together.'

'Ok, if you insist, I'll 'ave the prawn cocktail.'

'Pizza, prawn cocktail, how boring.'

'Well, the rest is in another language.'

Desmond opted for arancini and steak in red wine sauce. He also ordered a bottle of red wine, after asking Amanda what type she wanted. 'It's no good asking me,' she replied, 'all I know is Chardonnay. That one looks nice, the one with straw on 'alf the bottle.' 'That's chianti,' he replied, 'a red, red goes better with steak actually.'

Amanda tried to talk above the accordion music. She related what had happened in her life over the past two days. Her clients, conversations with family, friends, and television programmes. Desmond spoke about his time at work.

'Raymond, said to me yesterday, "If we don't get this order sorted out, we'll be in the pickies,"' the flesh on his forehead creased.

This brought an outburst of laughter from Amanda. 'They're stinging nettles,' she said through gulps of laughter.

'Oh, I thought it was a reference to the English term to be in a pickle. As I've said before, you have your own language in Aedre, no wonder you can't speak Italian menu.'

The waiter brought their starters, followed by their mains, when he noticed their empty plates.

'How are the two freedom fighters?' asked Desmond.

'Oh fine. They've gone out somewhere today, looking for wallpaper.'

'Something to match a picture of Mao Zedong?'

'Mousey tongue?'

'Mao Zedong,' Desmond laughed. 'Mousey tongue,' he shook his head.

'Who's that then? Someone off a children's programme?'

Desmond spluttered with laughter. 'I was just recovering from Mousey tongue. Chairman Mao, he was a socialist revolutionary, who ruled China.'

'Well if you will speak about these political people. You're as bad as Wayne and Anita. Mam asked her the other night when she was going to 'ave a child. "Steady on now Mair," she said, "We are not planning on having any, at the moment." "Well you don't want to leave it too long," Mam says.'

'I bet that went down well.'

'"Well there's other things to do, see Mair." "Like what," Mam says. "Well there are people suffering see." "Well you can't do anything about that." "That's just it. People seeing Jews being herded to German concentration camps, said there was nothing we could do. That's exactly what they did do. Nothing." My dad starts then, "All these protest marches don't achieve anything. This government isn't going to take any notice. They couldn't care less." Anita knows better now though, to start going on about what miners achieved and the improvement in working conditions. Her and my dad are both stubborn.'

'She's a strong woman ain't she? Wayne wants someone like that. It would be no good him marrying someone whose only ambition was to be married and have children.'

'We 'aven't finished yet love,' Amanda said to an approaching waiter.

The waiter handed her a long, narrow gift box.

'What's this,' Amanda's features were creased in puzzlement.

'Open it,' Desmond thanked the waiter.

Amanda opened the box, and took out a pendant, with a pink crystal stone.

'It's beautiful,' her eyes were wide, as she stared at the pendant in her palm.

'I'm glad you like it. I went into a few jewellers, but when I saw that one, I thought, that's the one.'

'Oh it is. Oh Desmond, I don't deserve someone like you,' Amanda's eyes were glistening with moisture.

'Of course you do,' Desmond took her hand across the table.

Dessert arrived, Amanda had ordered trifle, which came with the obligatory three raspberries. The wine was making it easier for Amanda to talk about her intimate feelings.

'It's quite dark in yere, innit?'

'Not as dark as it will be in the cinema.'

'I used to be scared of the dark when I was younger. I used to 'ave a small bedside light on all night. Now, I'm no longer afraid of the dark since meeting you, because black is beautiful,' she grinned.

'Our love surpasses hatred. It is the light that shines in this darkness,' Desmond raised his glass of wine.

Amanda listened raptly, to the generous words flowing across the table from Desmond. She languished in his presence. She thought again of how different Desmond was from any of the other boys she had known. Boys who would put on a show, trying to be something they weren't. Talking about how fit they were. The antics they got up to with their friends, how much they could drink. She looked at the clouds of froth floating on top of her coffee. Once the coffee had been drunk, Amanda excused herself, as she wanted to touch up her makeup in the ladies' room. She walked between two faux palm plants to reach the toilets. There were Mediterranean murals on the walls, and other Italianate pretensions. She noticed in the mirror, the purple stain around her lips. When that happened through drinking blackcurrant cordial, her father would say, 'Remember the black and white Minstrels. Well, she looks like the negative.'

Desmond had paid the bill when she returned to the table.

'We'll need to get going, if we are to make the afternoon performance,' he said. They left the restaurant, and Amanda was happy with wine and joy.

The cinema smelt of popcorn and peanuts. Desmond offered to buy popcorn, which Amanda declined, she patted her stomach, and said she could not eat another thing, not even a wafer-thin mint. The film was a comedy, at which Amanda laughed more than she could ever remember laughing before. She laughed for the wonderful meal, the museum which she had never thought to visit, the sun in the sky that day, and the man beside her. The day was evaporating when they emerged blinking from the cinema.

'I don't want this day to end,' Amanda said wistfully, holding onto Desmond on the platform, whilst waiting for her train to arrive.

'We'll see each other soon,' Desmond consoled.

'Not soon enough,' Amanda buried her face in Desmond's chest. She was tangled up in love. 'I don't want to go back there. Why can't people see how wonderful you are?'

Desmond held her as if holding her would heal her.

'We don't 'ave any trouble yere,' Amanda continued, 'Nobody stares at us, like we're planning to rob a bank or something, or shout 'orrible things at you.'

'Oh, they do,' Desmond said gently, 'we're up against the white establishment, wherever we go.'

Chapter 9

Desmond pulled into a cul de sac of detached, new build houses. There was a circular patch of rubble in the middle of the cul de sac. Some building machinery still lay about the site. The circular patch would be in a round lawn of grass next year. A patch of grass, meant to give an air of affluence. An attempt to make the deprivation of Aedre disappear. Desmond wondered why the supervisor had invited him to his house. What ulterior motive lay behind this visit? Was he to get the sack? Raymond, the supervisor, must have registered his confusion when inviting him. 'Just a general chat,' he had tried to reassure, 'I have them now and again with the workers.' He had asked Neil about it, 'You're privileged,' he said. 'He asks some of us to his house now and again. I think it's to get info from us.' 'I ain't no spy,' Desmond stepped back. 'Chill,' Neil put a hand on his shoulder, 'nothing like that. He won't expect you to grass on your teammates.'

'I wonder if it's anything to do with my work. I've been meeting targets, but he could find an excuse to sack me if he wants. I know some here don't like me cause I'm black.'

'He's not gonna sack you,' Neil said, as if he'd had suggested something ridiculous, like there were dinosaurs living on the Sceard mountain. 'There's laws against sacking people because of their colour these days.'

'He's not gonna give my colour as the reason is he?' Desmond said sarcastically

'He's gotta have a good reason,' Neil reassured. 'If he tried anything like that, Wayne and his lot will be on the case like a ton of bricks.'

Desmond however, was reaching that stage when there seemed little point in fighting. He was never going to be accepted. There was resistance now from Amanda's parents. He was tired of all these years of trying to adjust to a white society. Being looked down upon. The taunts, the insults. All the anger and resentment he had suppressed, was now beginning to surface.

Desmond stood in the doorway, under a portico, looking at the push button of the bell. He flipped a hand through his hair before ringing. He cleared his throat on hearing the click of the door being opened. A woman of around Raymond's age stood before a generous hallway. She was about five foot five, with shoulder length light brown hair, and was wearing a pair of wide flared cream trousers, a bold patterned blouse of a shiny material, and a long string of what Desmond took to be fake pearls.

'Hello, you must be Desmond,' she said pleasantly and smiled. 'I'm Gail,' she extended a hand.

'Pleased to meet you,' Desmond shook her hand.

'Do come in, Raymond is just in here.' She led him past the stairway, into a room that looked like an advert out of a magazine, used by a department store to sell furnishings. The colour scheme of this long room, was beige, cream and brown. There were some lacquered cream coloured side cabinets, on top of which were some ornaments of stone or gold finish, of an undecipherable shape. There was a wedding photo, some photos of a child from a baby to about four years of age. The room smelt of polish and perfume.

'Hello Desmond, it's great to see you,' Raymond rose from an armchair, shook Desmond's hand firmly and indicated the armchair opposite, in which Desmond sat upright.

'Can I get you anything?' there was a ring to Gail's voice, 'Tea, coffee?'

'He doesn't want tea or coffee,' Raymond said with mock derision. 'This is a man's meeting, get him something stronger,' Raymond opened the drinks cabinet.

'No thanks Mrs Wilson, I'm ok.'

'Oh, call me Gail. Anyway, you'll have to excuse me, I've just put Samuel to bed, so I have a chance to catch up on things I can't do with a five-year-old running around,' she said on leaving the room.

'Right, what will you have?' Raymond asked. He was dressed in green canvas trousers, an open-necked brown and cream checked shirt, and brown lace-up shoes. 'Whisky, rum, port.'

'I'm driving,' Desmond held up his palms.

'Well you must have a glass of wine at least. I have an excellent Sauvignon Blanc,' he took out two cut glass crystal wine glasses. 'The thing with Sauvignon, is to always go for an expensive bottle. Not this five-pound rubbish. You're wasting your money.'

He handed Desmond a glass of clear liquid, with a few bubbles clinging to the sides. Raymond sank into the opposite armchair, and reclined back.

'A nice place you have here Ray,' Desmond said whilst looking around the room. He was sitting on the edge of his chair, elbows on his knees.

'The success you see here, is the failure you don't.' He waited a while before continuing. 'So tell me Desmond, how are things going with you?' Raymond asked amicably.

'Do you mean in work or general?' Desmond said guardedly.

'Both'

'Work is fine,' there was a little tension in Desmond's voice.

'And family?' Raymond lent forward slightly.

'Yes, family is fine too.'

'You don't speak about your family much.'

'Nothing much to say, we keep ourselves to ourselves.'

'Best way sometimes, best way,' Raymond nodded, 'and girlfriends, is there anyone special?'

'There is someone.'

'Is that Neil's sister?'

Desmond gave him a guarded look.

'I don't go around with my eyes and ears closed,' Raymond said. 'I see you with someone lunchtime.'

'Yes, her name's Amanda.'

'Nice girl. I've met her a few times. She used to come along to the children's party. All the factories would club together around Christmas, and put on a party for the children. Yes, nice girl.'

'Yes, she is,' Desmond's gaze was fixed on Raymond, but his face was not displaying any emotion.

'To get back to work then,' there seemed to be a touch of frustration in Raymond's voice, as he took a sip from his glass

'Are you trying to tell me my work has been affected since I've been with Amanda?' Desmond said with some hostility.

'Not at all,' Raymond said hastily, 'in fact, your output has always been, and remains high.'

Desmond remained silent.

'To cut to the chase then,' Raymond said.

'Please do.'

'You see, profits from the factory have been doing well,' Raymond looked at Desmond, who gave no encouragement. 'So, we are looking at expanding.'

'Expanding. How? The Aedre factory, or opening others.'

'Well, we're not entirely sure yet,' Raymond appeared to be floundering a little.

'So, what you're saying is, that you want me to work elsewhere.'

'No, no,' Raymond flapped his free hand. 'You are happy in Aedre, aren't you?' a troubled look creased Raymond's features.

'Yes, I am, so what's all this about?

'Well,' Raymond said uncomfortably, 'Mr Roberts will be moving on, and it's been suggested I take his place.'

'What has that got to do with me, are you asking me for reassurance?'

'Well,' Raymond hunched his shoulders for a second, and looked away momentarily, 'if I take his place,' Raymond said slowly, 'my position will need to be filled.'

'And you're asking me to recommend someone?'

'Well,' Raymond said hesitatingly, 'I was thinking you may like to take it.'

'ME?!' Desmond gaped.

'Yes'.

'Why?' Desmond asked warily.

'Because you're one of the best workers.'

'Expansion,' Desmond sat back and let out a long breath, 'progression.'

'Yes,' Raymond nodded vigorously.

'Oh, I get this.' Desmond leaned forward, returning his elbows to his knees. Raymond looked confused. 'The token nigger. Look how progressive we are, we have promoted a black person.'

'That's not the way at all,' Raymond said incredulously. He had difficulty making full eye contact. 'As I said,' he was fumbling over his words, 'you are one of my best workers.'

'One!'

'The best.'

'The best, as the slave owner said, so, I'm your best slave.'

'Definitely not,' Raymond was taken aback, 'if that was the case, I would hardly be offering you my best wine.'

'No, you would just take the strap to me,' Desmond's voice was thick with bitterness.

'Why such resentment?' Raymond's face puckered with perplexity. 'I respect you, not only are you hard working, you're a decent guy. I'm not like some of the others. I detest the way some of them speak to you. In fact, I've had words with them about it.'

Desmond stared at him blankly.

'I said to them the other week,' Raymond talked on, a little flustered. 'I've had enough of the way you are referring to him. The names you're calling him, Sambo, Big Lips.' He glanced at Desmond, only to be met with a passive stare. 'Now,' he wagged his finger at no one, 'he was born in Wales, so that makes him Welsh.'

'And how do you think they are going to take it, when they hear I've been offered the supervisor's job?' Desmond was calm now.

'Give them time, give them time. Rome wasn't built in a day. You can't whitewash the world overnight. It doesn't work like that,' the impatience returned to Raymond's voice. 'Life doesn't fall into neat little packages.'

'They'll never accept me,' Desmond said wearily, 'not the workforce, Amanda's family,' there was a silent pause. 'Well, thanks for the wine,' Desmond went to stand up, 'I best be on my way.'

'Wait, not so soon. You've been here less than an hour.'

'I don't see much point in prolonging this.'

'Why are you turning down this opportunity for promotion? I don't understand it,' Raymond looked baffled. 'Do you want to be stuck on the factory floor for ever. What is it you want from life?'

'What makes you tick Ray. What turns you on?'

'Well, that's a bit personal,' Raymond looked embarrassed.

'I mean, what turns you on to life?

'I'm not sure what you're getting at,' Raymond's eyebrows creased towards each other.

'What makes you want to get up in the morning. What thrills you?'

'I have a comfortable life. I love my wife, and have a beautiful house and son.'

'Comfortable is not good enough Ray. I need more than comfort. You know,' Desmond settled back into the chair, 'a white woman once went up to Malcom X, and said, "How can I help your cause Mr X, what can I do?" and she was full of enthusiasm, and he just looked at her, and said "Nothing,"' Desmond paused. 'She didn't have the fire in her belly. She hadn't suffered the way us black people had. I listen to Lenny at work sometimes, when he thinks I can't hear him. And he's spouting off all that British National rubbish, and although I hate it, at least he has passion.'

'I wish he'd show some of that passion in his work,' Raymond said with disdain.

'The Black Panthers, they inspired many other activists. They had that hunger, to do something.'

'That's not the way,' Raymond said scathingly, 'violence and rioting.'

'Unfortunately, that was the only way. The state was taking up arms against them. It was endemic in America; it was the only way they knew. And so, the only way to fight violence is with violence,' there was an ardour to Desmond's voice.

'Didn't Martin Luther King preach non-violence?'

'Oh yes, but the black people were dissatisfied with the failure to tackle police brutality. What could they do, the Ku Klux Klan were also using such force against them?'

'But what has it achieved Desmond?' Raymond asked tiredly, 'Many of your race are still considered the underclass. You have a chance to change that. Take the job, show what black people can achieve. How can Amanda's family then say you are a failure? You would have achieved more than Neil. To say you have failed, would be to say that Neil has also.'

'Don't underestimate the passion of a black man, Ray.'

'Bit sexist isn't it?

'Black person then. You can see it in everything we do. You can see it in the way we dance. Have you ever loved a woman to the extent that she is all you think about for most of your day? She is on your mind when you go to bed at night, and the first thing on your mind when you wake up in the morning? That is something worth fighting for.'

'To make that woman happy, you will need to give her the material things she wants,' Raymond sneered.

'Then it is not love then.'

'You may think that now, but believe me, years down the line, when the infatuation has gone, it is the nice house, car and steady income women want.'

'Don't put all women in the same superficial category.'

Raymond let out a long, audible sigh. 'I was once like you. A young man, thinking I knew everything, and had the world at my feet. Life was an adventure that stretched out before me. Then one day you realise, you are not going to be a sports star, or great explorer, spending your life travelling around the world or changing the world. You look around and see what you have got, and you learn to appreciate it. My advice to you, and take it from someone who's been there, is to grab every opportunity you can, as it may not come your way again.'

Desmond stood up, and put his hand on Raymond's shoulder. 'You're a good guy Raymond, and I'm glad you're happy, but you have no idea of what makes me happy.'

'Do you?' Raymond looked directly at Desmond, and held his gaze, as they stared at each other in silence for a few minutes, before Raymond shouted to Gail. 'Gail, Desmond's leaving now,' as he led him to the door.

'Oh, I'm so sorry I have not been able to speak to you much,' Gail appeared from a room adjoining the hall.

'No worries Gail, thank you for letting me into your beautiful house,' Desmond said flatteringly.

'You're very welcome. Please come here again.'

'That would be lovely, goodnight.'

'You see Desmond,' Raymond said seriously, at the opened door, out of earshot of Gail, as Desmond stood in the front garden, which was illuminated by street and house security lights. 'There is something broken in racists. They are preyed upon, and drawn in.'

Chapter 10

Amanda stood watching the rain travel down the kitchen window in rivulets. The view outside was distorted by heat from the gas cooker, and steam from the kettle, which was now boiling to a crescendo. She sat down with her mug of instant Nescafé, at a small table near the window. The rain was coming down so thickly, it was impossible to see the end of the garden. Leaves and twigs floated down the path. The water carrying the leaves and twigs, was the colour of dishwater. A bucket her father used for gardening was rapidly filling, until rain could be seen bouncing off the horizontal round surface of water.

Amanda took a sip of warm, comforting coffee. She was still in her pyjamas and dressing gown, when she vaguely heard the church clock sing out the Sunday hour. Neil's mug was still on the table. His tea half drunk, and two semi-circular chunks were missing from his toast, which had been tossed to the side of his plate. The room smelt of roasting meat and boiling vegetables, an aroma that permeated the whole ground floor, and would last throughout the day, to the following Monday morning. Amanda passively watched the paving stones of the patio become darker, as the rain became heavier. Bouncing off the surface with such force, it was as if it was trying to reach the ground beneath. A need to water the soil, or digging for dusty diamonds. The sky was also the colour of stone. Clouds like lumps of grey granite blocked the sky. The raindrops disappeared into the thirsty lawn.

She could hear Neil in the next room cursing every object he touched. She could feel his anger, at every click of a light switch or turn of a newspaper page. If only this rain could dampen their anger towards Desmond. Rust the knives they wished to plunge into his soul. She thought back to the black doll her grandmother had bought her, as a child. Was this an attempt to ensure she would not grow up with any racial prejudice? Or was it just lip service? The chocolate doll her father had called it. She saw her first black man a few months later, in a queue at the bakery. He seemed as tall as a giraffe. His lips were swollen and brown, not pale and pink. They looked as if they had been carved from the bark of a tree. His hair was as black and glossy as shining coal. 'Look Mam,' she had said, 'there's a chocolate man.' A comment the man tried to ignore, embarrassed Mair, but brought a supressed smile to the lips of the other customers.

Voices from the lounge drifted into the kitchen. 'What a day', she heard her mother say, 'I 'ope it's not going to be like this all day.'

'Nah, supposed to clear up about one,' she heard Neil reply.

Thank goodness for that Amanda thought, the alternative of being stuck in the house all day did not thrill her.

'To think in some parts of the world they pray for rain like this,' she heard Wayne say.

She was meeting Nigel that afternoon. A meeting which she was looking forward to. Looking forward to a bit of calmness. There had been arguments all week over Desmond. This was not supposed to happen. She was meant to marry a white guy, and have two or three white children. Live happily in a little house somewhere in Aedre. 'This is all your fault,' her mother would admonish Neil. 'What did you want to bring 'im yere for?'

'Hang on a minute. It's not my fault. I didn't expect 'im to go after my sister, or that she would be interested in 'im even.'

'It's disgusting, we treated 'im with hospitality, and this is what he does.'

'Never trust them,' would come Gerald's voice from the armchair, 'they are not like us.'

'Well he had you eating out of his hand,' Neil retorted to Mair.

'Ooooh, if I had known what he was up to.'

After showering and dressing, Amanda closed the door of her bedroom to shut out the voices drifting up the stairs. She sat on the edge of the bed, alone with her love, her bare feet dangling. She stared impassively at the pale pink walls. Her spirits dampened by rain and gloom. At the curling picture of a boy band taken from some magazine, and stuck to the wall with scotch tape. Three shelves stacked with books and cuddly toys, which over the decades, had become encrusted with dust. She stood up, took a small cuddly rabbit down from the shelf. The one Desmond had bought her for Easter, holding a red satin heart between its paws. She turned it over in her hands, as if handling a relic. The dressing table, the surface of which was crammed with accoutrements, adolescent essentials, such as perfume, make up, moisturiser, and a jewellery box so full she could not close the lid. Samson's ears horned up, on hearing the sound of Amanda's movement. He was curled up on a pale grey beanbag in the corner. He stood up, stretched, repositioned himself and closed his eyes. She sat back down on the bed and hugged her knees towards her chest and turned her body, until she was fully on the bed, comforted by the sensation of soft, thick duvet under her feet. She was level with the window overlooking the garden. The rain was by now a light drizzle, but the wind was giving life to trees, dustbins and discarded papers. The concrete clouds must have tipped their surplus water, and were now moving on to drier climes. A grey light flooded the room, but it was not an optimistic greeting.

The punishment for a night's drinking spree was a throbbing stomach churning the next morning. She had not drunk much last night however, so why did she feel so bad? She had spent Friday night at the house with Anita, drinking lager out of coffee mugs. They had watched a film Anita had on tape, called *Dirty Dancing*, which they had seen at least three times before, but it was a light-hearted, feel-good film, which Amanda felt she needed at that point in time, after Anita had spoken to her of some racial injustices.

'I read an article on the treatment of aborigines once, and I couldn't believe that a report came out in the seventies, seventies mark you,' Anita dumbfoundedly pointed at Amanda. 'In 1969 the aboriginal race was officially recognised as Homo sapiens.'

'What?'

'I know, I had to read it again. The original settlers treated the aborigines diabolically. Some still do today, but there was a case where an aboriginal man was shot, and his wife tried to escape up a tree, and they were shooting at the woman in the tree, and *laughing*!'

'Disgusting.'

'I know, and white settlers called that civilisation!'

Desmond had been out celebrating a friend's birthday that night, and he was busy the rest of the weekend, doing things for the family. Amanda wondered however whether that was just an excuse. She was glad of Anita's company, as she could speak to Anita about her situation. Anita and Wayne were the only ones standing by her, against the family. More so Anita, as Wayne just took things in his stride, and was reluctant to pursue arguments. Anita was more vocal, 'Well Amanda,' she had voiced, 'despite all the setbacks, you have stood by Desmond. Good for you.'

She had spent a quiet night out with Sharon last night, and had come home early, despite Sharon's protestations. She had no desire to go to the rugby club or another rave. She saw from the window, the light glinting off rain washed slate roofs. There was a soft tap on the bedroom door.

'Can I come in?' Neil said softly, and she recognised the tone.

'Ok.'

Amanda sat back on the edge of her bed, as Neil cautiously walked across the room, like Samson when stalking a bird or morning leaf. He sat on the bed beside her. How quickly she had grown up he thought. It was like missing a bus, and watching it roll down the village. If only he had seen this.

'I was worried,' he continued gently, 'as you 'ave been up yere a long time.'

Amanda looked morosely at the dark shadows cast across the carpet, by the increasing light from the window.

'I just wanted some quiet,' Amanda said neutrally.

'I can remember when you were born.'

'You were only four,' she said tonelessly.

'Yeah, but I can still remember it. I can remember it, as until then I was the centre of attention. That's it now I thought. Everybody will be wanting the new baby.'

Amanda remained silent, staring at the carpet.

'The week before you were born, Mam was showing Aunty Vi all the presents which had been bought. Aunty Vi was always telling Mam off for spoiling me. When Mam left the room, Aunty Vi tapped the side of my nose and said, "Your nose is being pushed out now."'

'That wasn't a very nice thing to say,' she said indifferently.

'Aunty Vi always thought boys shouldn't be spoilt. When I had a tantrum, she would glare at me, "Boy's shouldn't scream," she would say, "It's not normal."'

A slight smile crept across Amanda's face.

'And then you were brought 'ome. Weighing just seven pounds four ounces. You were put on the sofa, and I felt so much love for you.'

'You felt like that at FOUR?!' Amanda said incredulously.

'Oh yeah. Some mornings, Wayne would go into your room, get you out of the cot and put you on one of our beds. Gave Mam a heart attack, "Where's the baby, where's the baby?" Neil clutched his hands to his chest, voice increased two octaves in mocking imitation of Mair. 'He had a right rollicking. "You could 'ave dropped her," Mam used to shout.'

Neil moved further back on the bed, so he was able to recline against the wall.

'We were with each other a lot, when we were growing up,' he resumed. 'Remember we used to jump over Mrs Haymer's wall?'

'Yeah,' Amanda's face brightened, 'We used to run up her garden path, thinking we were being really daring. What was that word Wayne used? Antarctic?'

'Anarchic.'

'That's it, we used to think we were being really hip and anarchic, jumping over someone else's wall, and running up their garden path.'

They both laughed.

'And when we were older, she was always moaning to Mam about us,' Amanda continued, a little more cheerfully.

Neil pretended to hold a telephone to the side of his face, 'Mair, Mair,' he mocked, 'there's kids on my property, and I think they're in connection with your sons.'

They both laughed again, Amanda propped herself up onto her elbows. The sadness had now gone from her eyes.

'Then there was that party, that Pugsy was supposed to 'ave,' Neil resumed.

'Oh yeah, I remember that,' Amanda's expression became lively. 'His parents were supposed to be away for the weekend, but they decided not to go. So all these kids turned up at his door, with cans of lager and cider. He was whispering to everybody on his doorstep, "Go up to Aedre Brook." So there were about twenty of us, all around Aedre Brook. We put the cans in the water to keep cool. Then Pugsy came along with a radio. We were all arguing about which station to play.' They laughed to the point they found difficulty breathing. 'We must 'ave looked right prats,' Amanda managed to say through her laughter, 'dancing by the side of the brook.'

'And there was that idiot doing the air guitar,' Neil jumped from the bed, and got down to the floor on his knees and lay back, playing an imaginary guitar.

'Oh stop, stop,' Amanda said through giggles.

'You snogged Tweetie that night,' Neil pointed to Amanda, with a wide smile across his face.

'Tweetie, yeah. Loads of girls had a crush on Tweetie,' Amanda said merrily. 'Sharon was crazy about 'im. He was going out with Nicola Thomas. Went out with her for about two years. I think they really liked each other. Sharon used to ask me to spy on them, "Was he with her in Aedre Youth on Friday?" she would ask. Look at the state of 'im now,' said Amanda. 'Fat.'

'And he'll be bald in a few years' time, like his old man.'

'Not like you though, you've got a thick mop on you,' she ruffled Neil's hair. 'Then there was that party at Wally's. He was playing his father's records.'

'That's right,' recognition lit up on Neil's face, as if a light switch had been flicked. 'The records he was playing were bloody awful. The cat danced in or something.'

'The cat danced in, and the cat danced out again. And there was Julia Mathews, dancing in and out of the door, with her wrists flopped out in front of her, pretending to be a cat. Julia, there's a nutter for you now.'

'And what was that record now?' Neil had returned to the bed, where he half lay. '"She ain't no snitch, and I love the way she pitch," what the hell does that mean?'

'I could write better lyrics than that,' Amanda laughed

'A five-year old could write better lyrics than that.'

'La, La, La, lalalala,' they both sang in unison.

'Minto asked 'im if he had any Run DMC. "Now does my dad look as if he's into Run DMC,"' Neil said, in imitation of Wally. They both took some moments to laugh.

'Oh, I've been to some parties in my time,' Neil recommenced. 'I went to one in Combfeld once, with Smithy and Drake. It was full of thirteen-year-olds, they were rolling about on the floor acting drunk. "There's lots of drink," I said. "Come on," Smithy said, "let's go. I don't like this. All this underage drinking. We could get into trouble." "Come and 'ave a look at this," Drake said. We went into the kitchen, and there were all these kids, mixing wine gums with water.'

Amanda shrieked with laughter. 'What did you want to go there for, you big kid?'

'I like our family,' Neil's voice became serious again. 'I want things to stay as they are.'

'Things must change, I suppose, but we'll always 'ave each other,' Amanda said mildly.

'I see things falling apart. Ever since I brought Des yere,' Neil said tightly. 'I rue the day I did that.'

'Oh come on,' Amanda stiffened, 'Des is great. He treats me well, he is kind and generous. I could do plenty worse. Why can't you all see 'ow 'appy he makes me?'

'He would be perfect,' Neil stopped for a few seconds, 'if he were white.'

'He can't 'elp the colour of his skin,' Amanda pleaded, 'any more than we can 'elp 'aving brown eyes. It's no sin to be black.'

'I know, but black and white don't mix,' Neil said sombrely. 'I hate what he's doing to you Mand.'

'What's he doing, apart from making me 'appy?'

'It's what people are saying.'

'Who?' Amanda sat upright.

'No respectable woman goes with a black man.'

'Who is saying that?' Amanda demanded.

'It's what people are thinking.' Neil looked away.

'So you're a mind reader now.'

'Isn't it obvious?' Neil snapped, 'if he cared about you, he wouldn't be doing this. Oh, he's doing alright for 'imself.' Neil stood up, and paced the room. 'He's managed to get 'imself a nice, good looking white woman.'

'Stop it,' Amanda covered her ears with her palms.

'He saw his chance alright,' Neil said forcefully, 'an innocent, naïve white girl. Others would turn 'im down, but no, yere was one who was too nice. Would not see his colour as an obstacle.'

'Will you stop saying things like that,' Amanda shouted.

Neil bent his knees to be eye level with her. Cupped his hands around her face. His voice became tender again. 'You can do so much better. A girl like you has so much going for you.'

'Go Neil. Just get out,' tears stung Amanda's eyes.

Neil walked towards the door, but stopped and turned before leaving. 'I can't stand what's 'appening to you,' he said.

Amanda got dressed in her room with the radio playing, to drown out any other household sounds. She stepped outside her room, on hearing Mair announce dinner was ready. She noticed the pale light from the narrow window stretched across the landing, and reluctantly made her way downstairs. She sat morosely through lunch, putting the minimum amount of food on her plate, avoiding eye contact. The skin around her eyes was puffy and sore. Mair and Wayne attempted to lighten the mood with easy conversation. Gerald would mutter and grunt his words, whilst Neil was mostly silent.

'You've 'ardly eaten anything,' Mair commented to Amanda.

'Never mind, more for us,' Wayne said, as he helped himself to more vegetables.

When the meal ended, Amanda stood in the garden to while away the time until she could leave to meet Nigel. She was grateful for the anaemic sunlight, poking through the curdling clouds, lifting the haze of thick gloom which had descended that morning. At least she and Nigel would be able to go out walking. There were the usual sounds of a Sunday. A dog barking in the distance, voices of relatives arriving or leaving. She looked at the tall, brown backs of the houses opposite. Separated from the house she lived in, by a narrow lane. This strip was once used by house owners to cross into neighbouring houses, and was considered safe for children to play in, as inaccessible to traffic. Children would race up and down on their tricycles. Now it was only used by sniffing dogs, or as a means of getting somewhere unseen. She could see over the wall to the garden next door. An assortment of weeds and vegetation had staggered over the garden, which had once been owned by Mr and Mrs Collins. Both of them had since passed away. Mr Collins had been a keen gardener, a practice continued by his wife, after his death, and her son and daughter in later years, when she became too weak to pull up the weeds. The house was now owned by a recently married couple, in their early twenties. The once well-tended garden, left to its own devices had become an impenetrable mass of nettles, and other shrubbery, ambushed by weeds.

Magpies were chattering away in their magpie monologues. The chattering became incessant, jarred by the caw of crows.

She looked up towards the direction of bird voices, and was surprised to see they were attacking a parrot. *Where on earth did that come from?* she thought. There used to be a parrot in the pet shop her father used to take her to, when she was very young. Her father would take her to see it every Saturday morning. He told her it had been painted. *Why do they attack it?* she shielded her eyes with the palm of her hand and followed the attack. Don't they realise it is just a bird like themselves? Jealousy doesn't exist in animals, so they cannot be jealous of its' pretty colours.

Chapter 11

Amanda reached the road at the bottom of the rows of streets, which was awash with rainwater. Turned into a lake almost, in which empty crisp packets, and chocolate wrappers floated. She could see the top of the pavement curb, where the gathering of rainwater was at its thinnest, and tentatively picked her way across the exposed edge, as if walking on a tightrope. She could hear the fizz of wet tyres from the main road. She decided to cut through the side streets to get to where she had arranged to meet Nigel, as the gradient of ground on that route, moved in an upwards direction.

Nigel was waiting for her at the corner of his street. Hands in his pockets, and blowing air into his cheeks. He smiled on seeing her approach.

'Hey, how's it going Tubbs?' he said cheerfully, using his pet name for her.

'Hey Tiggs,' she responded, using another form of his nickname, 'am I glad to see you.'

'It's not that bad, surely?'

'Don't you believe it. Neil 'as been bloody awful to me all weekend. I'll be glad to go to work tomorrow.'

'What's Prince Charming been up to now? He's going out with Rosaline, isn't he?'

'Yeah, well, she doesn't seem to be making 'im 'appy. I've a good mind to ring her up and tell her to get round there and cheer 'im up.'

'I was surprised, I didn't think she was his type.'

'A lot of people are saying that, but she's a lovely girl.'

'Yeah, but not Neil's type of lovely. Maybe with Wayne getting married, you with Desmond, he feels he's getting left behind.'

'Maybe, but I'm still worried. He's my brother, and I adore 'im, but he is a bit of a love them and leave them type, and I don't want Rosaline getting hurt.'

'He went out with Donna on and off for two years.'

'Yeah, until she went to uni and met someone else.'

'Ave you spoken to Ros about it?'

'Aven't had a chance, they've only just started going out with each other. She rang me just over a week ago, saying she had served Neil, he was in there buying a packet of crisps. He started talking to her, and "Guess what?" she said all gushing, "He asked me out." She thought he had just gone in there to see her, as he could 'ave bought the crisps in Phil's store, and wouldn't 'ave 'ad to queue.'

'Poor sod. I bet she was excited; he'd be quite a catch for her.'

'What about you? Time you settled down isn't it?'

'Looking for the right girl ain't I?' he smiled cheekily.

'Well you may find that you are not the right boy for the right girl. Anyway, where are we going?

They stopped at the end of another street. The air was hazy with moisture, and the sky was pockmarked by clouds. The rain however, seemed to have spent itself dry.

'We both 'ave walking shoes on,' Nigel said. 'We've both come prepared, so why not try walking up the mountain? Should be ok on the mountain path.'

'Why not?' Amanda shrugged.

They walked through some more of the many streets that had expanded around the main road. Nigel was wearing a Pac-a-Mac, which squeaked when he moved his arms. They passed people who had nowhere to go, other than their front door.

'People are born, and will die in these 'ouses,' Nigel said. 'My grandmother will be one of them.'

'And mine. Wayne says coal is the only reason these 'ouses were built. Miners' 'ouses were built for function, not ornamentation. He says the villages now 'ave a diminished role, in the productive economy or something. Last week he came out with, "The coal industry is now fossilising into myth."'

'Bit deep innit. Is he practising to become the Chancellor of the Exchequer or something?'

'He's union mad. 'Im and Anita. They're a pair well matched there. I wouldn't want to go around to their 'ouse, when they're married. It will be like the *Politics Now* show.'

'My mother likes Wayne. "He's a nice lad that Wayne," she used to tell Karen. "He won't pass you by on the road, without saying 'ello." My father would start then, "Aye, I see 'im down the Dragon after work on a Friday. He has one or two pints, and that's his lot." I think my Mam was 'oping he and Karen would get married.'

'Fat chance of that 'appening. She would need a degree in politics to understand 'im. "These mountains were skinned by men hunting profits," he would say. "Expanding as far as money and nature would permit. A massive experiment in coal mining." "Ho, shut up with your posh talk," my father would say, "provided jobs didn't it. What 'ave we got now?" "Fresh air for one thing,"' Amanda gave a mocking imitation of Wayne's voice. '"What are you?" she lowered her voice to represent Gerald, '"One of Thatcher's army?"'

'I bet that went down well,' Nigel laughed through puffs of breath.

'That sets Wayne off about exploitation. Be thankful you don't 'ave to listen to that.'

'It's bliss now Karen has left. Bathroom is tidy, there are biscuits in the tin. No stupid soaps on the tele.'

They went through an alley between the bulging walls at the ends of back gardens. There were what looked like sentry boxes at the ends of some gardens, which had once been outdoor toilets. The end house had a long crack down its side, caused by coal subsidence. Even the houses could not escape the coal industry. They passed a pub, where the ground outside was littered with squashed cigarette ends. A man in his late thirties was standing to the side of the entrance, crushing the last part of his cigarette under the sole of his shoe.

'Awright Butt,' he smiled, showing discoloured, smoke-wrecked teeth as they neared. 'What's the score then?' his voice roughened by years of nicotine inhalation.

'Don't know, 'aven't been watching the match,' Nigel shrugged.

'It's no good asking me about football,' Nigel said, once out of hearing range of the man. 'The only reason I knew the European football had started last year was because *Only Fools* was not on the tele.'

'Good job it's not Wales playing rugby, otherwise he would 'ave thought you were really odd.'

'I'm still not interested. A win isn't going to improve my life.'

The houses ended abruptly, and they found themselves at the allotments. The allotments were made up of ugly makeshift buildings. Rough craftsmanship, enterprises in wood, recycled doors and nails. Planks precariously held together by wire. One such edifice housed homing pigeons. A large sack, full of onion bulbs leaned against one of the sheds. Fat globes, waiting to be planted.

'Those are Matty's fathers,' Nigel pointed to the pigeon shed. 'He wanted to put them in the back garden, but Matty's mother wouldn't 'ave it.'

'Hannah's neighbour keeps pigeons in the back garden, much to her mother's annoyance.'

'My grandfather used to 'ave an allotment yere. He was proud of his horticulture. His vegetables were a work of art. He won prizes with his carrots. His garden also, he loved his begonias. Only sheep would regularly trample on his front lawn, and raid the flower beds. A passing kid used to think it was funny to open the back-garden door, so sheep could get in, until he put a bolt on it. He never moves from his armchair in front of the TV now.'

They were crossing a field to get to the mountain path. There was a discarded carcass of a car in the middle of the pasture, which looked as if it had fallen from the sky. A rusty old car, decomposing in the field. Streams, satiated with rainwater, a rain which fed the mountains, propelled downwards by gravity towards the river. Sprinting over small rocks on its course. Some of the streams were temporary, and would disappear when the weather dried. The grass was gleaming and treacherous. Their feet were sinking slightly into the sodden ground, exposing the claylike soil underneath, which was the colour of milk chocolate. They were glad to reach the solidity of the dirt track. They looked up at the land which had been squeezed into mountains. Mountains refreshed by rain, which gave the earth a biscuity aroma. Raindrops, which the earth had been waiting for, would fizzle the dust of the parched track in summer, and would remind Amanda of sherbet on her childhood tongue. The enormity of the mountains provided a heroic backdrop to the village. Now here she was, a character in a passion play, only she did not know her next line.

Their pace was becoming gradually slower, as they climbed the gradient of the track. The land had been mercilessly assaulted by erosion. Weathering had picked out weaker aspects of the land, and had eroded, rendering parts easier to navigate. The surface either side of the tapering track looked like a rough sea. Small rock outcrops, and tufts of parched grass swayed in the wind, like swelling waves. Plants clothed the land, and flora was tucked between the angular rocks protruding through the coarse grass.

They stopped to catch their breath, and looked down at the side of the mountain they had just climbed. From here they could see the shape of history. A defunct winding tower clung savagely to the side of the mountain, like acne clinging to a flawless complexion. Coal, the most important contribution geology had made to entrepreneurialism in the village. The past cannot be obliterated, and here was a reminder of an industry which had once blighted the landscape.

'I love this place,' Amanda said. 'Yere are where my friends are. People of substance.'

They stood side by side, gazing at the village below them. The bottom part of the slope was crammed with brick and layers of slate. Slate roofs provided a covering of scales to the houses.

'But I may need to get away from yere,' she continued

'Where will you go to?' they both kept staring at the distant houses below them.

'I don't know, Jamaica maybe.'

'Will things be any different there?'

'It's got to be better than yere.'

'It's totally different, to suddenly up and change your life. It's not as if you could catch a bus 'ome and see your Mam.'

'Desmond will never be accepted yere, no matter where we go in this country, there will always be some racism.'

'I'm sure there will be problems in Jamaica, maybe of a different sort. You may be the one in the minority then. I don't think it will be all sea and palm trees. You won't know anyone. I don't think you can run away from your problems that easily.'

'I wonder if they sell Milky Ways in Jamaica.'

'Doubt it, maybe Mango Ways.'

'Oh look, yere comes Nat,' Amanda pointed to a boy of their age, walking up the track towards them, holding a bunch of flowers.

'Hey Nats, where you going with those?' shouted Nigel. 'Aven't got a secret girl somewhere, 'ave you?'

'I'm going to the cem, putting flowers on my mother's grave.'

'Aw, they're lovely,' Amanda enthused.

'Gina not going with you?' Nigel asked.

'Naw, she's keeping an eye on Aleisha. Watching a video, *Aladdin* or something.'

'Ow's your old man?'

'He's ok. His brother and sister call in often. I'm gonna cut across yere to get to the cem.'

'See you and Gina at the Futures next Fri?'

'Yeah, see you both,' he waved.

'Poor sod. You put your foot in it, didn't you?' Amanda rolled her eyes.

'He'll be alright. Probably give me stick over it.'

'He's a nice boy. Gina did alright for herself there. Good job he 'as Gina mind. 'Elp 'im get over it, and she's good with Aleisha. Come on, we best get going if we want to get back before dark.'

124

They turned their backs on the village to continue up the last part of the mountain, before the peak. They now saw the endless grass and trees, stretching towards the sky. The trees were still dripping from the morning rain. The grass either side of the track became soft and hairy, a bit like Rosaline's sister's hair, when she used to gel it up. The sun was now looking over the mountain, as they made their way over exposed tree roots, spread like fingers over the track, which had now dwindled to nothing. Two options presented themselves. They could either turn back, or carry on to the top of the mountain. A sea of ferns rippled in the breeze. Purposeful partings petered out into long grasses, or bare stretches of mountainside.

'It would be easy to get lost yere, especially if tempted to stray,' Amanda said.

'Well we are not going to do that, because we know better. Besides, I doubt we will get lost, as we've explored these mountains since childhood. I think we made the track. We used to come and play yere, all of us. Wore the grass down. Now a new track is being made, by the next gang of kids.'

They negotiated the mountain easily, following the track to the mountain height, clambering over earth softened with moisture. Nothing was unexpected to them, despite being slippery with rain. Gorse climbed over the land, and straggling bramble bushes tried to cling to anything which got within their grasp. Damp had intruded, and cushions of moss had made a spongy floor. The wind was so strong at that high point, it was as if the mountain itself was exhaling, and reaching a crescendo, where conifers and ferns burst into movement, illustrating the fluid shape of the wind. Trees here were like the tower of Pisa, and bushes were almost horizontal. They watched the trees dancing like at a discotheque, sun strobing between moving branches. They finally reached the summit of the mountain, where they stood buffeted by the winds. The mountains gave isolation. Gossip would seep through gaps under doors, or through letterboxes with the mail, down in the villages, but here, all that could be escaped.

The sky was now hidden again by cloud, which had pushed the sun behind a veil. They looked at the mountain opposite, where the sky and ground appeared to be merged into a wet, silvery grey. They stood side by side, chests heaving in unison.

'We don't want to be staying yere too long,' Nigel said, staring straight ahead.

The walk down the mountain was easier, and took half the time than the ascent. When they reached the streets however, the damp, grey day was drifting into darkness.

Chapter 12

'He's in there now with the boss again,' Paul, more commonly referred to as Lenny, strutted self-assuredly in front of his co-workers, who were working behind their benches.

'That's the fourth time in three weeks.' His six-foot, lean frame continued to move arrogantly up and down the rows of benches. The sleeves of his checked shirt were rolled up to his elbows, exposing tattoos. His thin legs covered by tight-fitting jeans, were also rolled half way up his calves, stopping just above Dr. Martens boots. His dark hair was cropped as short as a barber's shaver would allow.

'You mark my words. He's gonna be given the supervisor's position soon, over us, and that's not fair.'

'Aw come on, he's alright. I'd rather 'ave 'im as the gaffer than some.'

'It's just because he's a Nigger, innit. They wanna show 'ow progressive they are.'

'Look,' said Stephen, who was known as Smithy, 'he's been working with us for three years, and he considers 'imself one of us.'

'Yeah, well he ain't is he,' Lenny said tightly through a narrow gap in his exposed teeth. 'If his brain was as big as his dick, he'd be running this place.'

'What's 'appened to you?' someone shouted from a workbench, further back from the floor. 'Been to one of those BNP meetings again.'

'It's the only place I can 'ear some sense.'

'SENSE! that load of shaven-headed idiots,' came another voice from somewhere on the factory floor, 'I'd 'ardly call them Oxford professors. Are you gonna get a swastika tattoo?'

'These villages 'ave been built on the blood, sweat and tears of miners,' Lenny stabbed a pointed finger to the ground, whilst continuing to swagger back and forth. 'After the war they came flooding yere,' Lenny had the attention of his co-workers, who had now put down their tools. He met their stares unflinchingly. 'But not to the villages. Not even the Romans got yere,' he said.

'I don't blame them,' said one of the workers.

'Bloody hell Lenny,' said another. 'What's got into you? They're quite civilised you know. They 'aven't got shields and spears.'

'Aye, what do they do at these BNP meetings, keep showing *Zulu*?' came another voice from the floor.

'Britain,' Lenny almost spat, 'this small little island,' he paused and looked at his co-workers, 'and we invited them in. Come on over, yere's an 'ouse for you. Sign on the dole. Take our money. The money our 'ardworking citizens 'ave earned,' Lenny again paused for effect. His audience looked at him in silence. The whir of the machinery being the only sound. 'The reason why Walty's sister can't get a flat,' he stabbed a finger in Walty's direction. 'She's not asking for an 'ouse. Just a one bedroomed flat in Brynhalig. And she can't even get that! And I'll tell you why,' he paused again, 'and I know a lot of you won't want to 'ear this. But I'm gonna say it anyway, as it needs to be said. The reason why our grandmothers can't get a decent place to live, and our brothers and sisters can't get jobs is because of Niggers and Pakis.'

'Aw come on now. You're getting out of order,' the work colleagues were now turning their heads to look at each other, before looking back to Lenny.

'Yeah, you're out of order,' Smithy admonished, 'his race has been downtrodden enough. Not only is he a good worker, he's a good bloke.'

'See, this is what I mean,' Lenny continued, 'you've been brainwashed by all this political correctness. Even the police are getting soft.'

'Aye, and you've been brainwashed by the BNP,' came a voice from the floor.

'You don't believe all that trash do you?' came another voice.

'My family lived on handouts during the strike,' Lenny pointed belligerently, his stare was bold. 'My father went around the 'ouses begging every Friday night,' he said emphatically.

'As did a lot around yere,' someone said.

'Fighting for his village,' Lenny was undaunted, 'and now the immigrant lot are trying to get into Aedre,' his eyes narrowed, mouth twisting around the words. 'Worming their way into our villages,' he prodded his thumb to his chest. He walked over to Neil, and stood in front of him, staring directly into his eyes, 'taking our women.'

'You're not going back to the strike are you?' Smithy said. 'We fought each other during that time. And I'm not talking about the police either. We fought our own.'

'Blacklegs weren't our own,' Lenny snapped. 'They deserved everything they got. My father 'ad three children to bring up.' He was fired up by passion. 'He would rather 'ave begged than go crawling before Thatcher,' Lenny shouted, eyes blazing.

'Give it a rest Lenny. No Thatch please,' shouted one of his colleagues.

'WE LOST,' another co-worker moved from behind his desk. The others were silent, chests heaving visibly. 'You 'ave to accept that.'

'So we just lie down and take it?' Lenny said aggressively. 'Give up the fight? The people of Aedre are far too proud for that. BNP is the voice of the people,' he held a raised fist in the air. 'Our country is being stolen from under our noses, and we need to take it back. This is WHITE country.'

A silence followed, in which Lenny's breath came in heavy, short gasps. The silence was broken by the sound of a slow hand clap. Everyone turned to the entrance, to see the clapping came from Desmond, who walked slowly onto the floor.

'Bravo. Quite a speech.' There was a pause, before Desmond continued. 'I hear your white voices,' Desmond's voice betrayed little emotion. He spoke calmly and steadily. On reaching the middle of the floor, he turned to face his co-workers. 'My parents came to this country to work and build it. They left the sun and colour of Jamaica to come here.'

Some of the workers stared at the floor, others stared blankly at Desmond.

'I had a dream,' Lenny muttered to the floor. Desmond shot him an angry glance, which Lenny caught from the corner of his eye, and went silent.

'They were crammed into a house with twenty others,' Desmond stopped to look at each of his co-workers. 'They had a small room, and shared the bathroom with the other twenty,' he paused again. 'So they came to Wales, as they were told to expect a warm welcome.' Another pause, 'Wales was renowned for its hospitality. My father worked every day at the docks. Doing the only jobs available to him and the other immigrants. The jobs no one else wanted to do. There were no signs in the windows or pubs, saying no Irish or blacks, but it was unsaid. They soon learned where they would not be welcomed though,' he stopped, to let this sink in. 'My older sister is a nurse. She works nine hour shifts to save lives.' Desmond raised his voice, 'So don't tell me we are coming here taking your handouts. We've earned our right to be British.'

'All right, you lot, now get back to work,' Raymond said irritably as he walked from his office onto the floor.

There was the sound of shuffling, as the workers picked up their tools.

'Aedre was built on immigration you idiot,' Neil muttered as Lenny walked past, but loud enough for Desmond to hear. He had a look of triumph on his face.

Chapter 13

'Come on Des, let's get out of this place. Let's go over the Drag,' Neil playfully punched Des lightly on the upper arm, at the end of their shift.

The acrid smell of spilt beer met them as soon as they opened the door to the Green Dragon. They walked through the lobby, the walls of which were plainly painted with what once may have been cream, but were now a nicotine stained yellow. There was a machine in one corner with slits for feeding in coins. A large black telephone, was attached to the opposite wall.

Neil pushed open a door to another room, from which he shouted to the barmaid, 'Is it ok if we come in Jan, because we're not wearing ties?'

'Anybody with a clean shirt is overdressed in this place,' came a voice from somewhere in the room.

They walked into a large room. The floor was tiled with vinyl and uncarpeted. One long wall was painted a deep green. The rest were the same colour as the walls in the lobby. There were many metal-framed windows on the other long wall, and some on the back wall. The space at the back was taken up by a pool table, around which two men in their late twenties were playing, watched by four others who sat drinking, on wooden chairs alongside the wall. A dartboard hung on one wall, and a TV screen on another. Apart from that, there was nothing else on the walls. A group of men, aged between late twenties to late fifties, sat around the TV screen, watching a football match, with pints of beer in one of their hands, and some with a cigarette in the other. Every now and again a cheer would emanate from the group, or a shouted complaint against the way a ball had been dealt with.

The rest of the room was filled with simple wooden chairs and tables. Three middle-aged men took up one table, who were dressed in a style that went out in the seventies. Four took up another, two of which were in their sixties. Some of the men had their sleeves rolled up to their elbows, exposing faded tattoos. One had large sparse teeth, which grew out of his gums like calcified deposits. Wisps of nicotine rose through the air. They nodded at Neil, as he walked in.

'Is there anybody you don't know?' Desmond asked.

'They've been coming yere since nineteen-forever,' Neil replied.

The bar was about ten feet long, and a solitary man in his mid-twenties, dressed in jeans and a donkey jacket was sat at the far end of the bar. His face was buried in a pint glass.

'Hey, how are things going Keg?' Neil stood alongside the man.

'Awright, what brings you yere on a Thursday night?'

'This is a work mate, Des. It's been a bloody awful day today, so we are in need of a pint.'

'Pleased to meet you, Butt,' Keg extended a hand to Desmond. 'The names Kevin, but call me Keg. What did you want to bring 'im to a dump like this for Nev?' Nev was a name some used for Neil. 'You could've taken 'im somewhere a bit better.'

'And what's wrong with this place?' the barmaid Jan said with mock indignation. 'At least you get a decent pint yere. Not watered down like some places, a beer squash, and we don't charge you an arm and a leg either.'

'You tell 'im Jan,' Neil said, 'who does he think he is, ay, Lord somebody.'

'Lord Muck maybe,' Jan wiped sticky patches off the part of the bar in front of them, with a damp cloth.

'What can I get you two gentlemen?'

'Huh, there's no gentlemen in yere,' Keg said with humorous cynicism.

'Watch it you,' Jan replied in jest, 'or you'll 'ave this wet cloth across your 'ead.'

'Ok, ok, no fighting talk now,' Neil held his palms up in front of him. 'We'll 'ave two pints of your best please Jan luv, meaning as Keg yere is not offering.'

'Who do you think I am, Rockefeller?'

'That's why he drinks yere,' Jan said, 'good beer at a decent price.'

'Not to mention the charming company and service,' Neil quipped.

'So, you didn't set 'im up then, like you did with that new apprentice?' said Keg.

'I've told you, he's had a hard day. Besides, it's not Russell serving. That was Scott,' Neil said to Desmond. 'When we first brought 'im yere, we told 'im to ask for a Bacardi and Coke. Russell the landlord said, "Now do we look as if we sell bloody Bacardi?"'

'That was mean,' Desmond grinned.

'You'd know when Russell is behind the bar,' said Keg, 'as soon as the door opens, he'd shout, "GET OUT."'

'Before he knew who was coming in?' the flesh above Desmond's eyebrows creased.

'And that's on a good day,' said Neil.

'Remember that posh bird you brought yere once?'

'You brought a posh girl here?' Desmond asked with consternation.

'Aye, she was 'ome from uni for Christmas. Me and Smithy bumped into her and her two friends, just outside. So we thought we'd show them how real people live 'round yere.'

'And were they impressed?'

'Probably had more fun yere than anywhere else they went that night.'

'I bet you didn't see her again though.'

'Nah, they went off to some poncy place. Anyway, where are you off to tonight?' he addressed Keg.

'I'm off down to that trendy place in Briog.'

'Well you could 'ave made a bit more of an effort with the clobber.'

'What's wrong with it? This is a clean shirt, put on tonight. I'm meeting Daz and the crowd. Me and Gill 'ave split up see. So I'm off on the pull.'

'Well you're not going to pull dressed like that.'

'I 'ear you're going with Rosaline.'

'News travels fast.'

'It's unpossible to keep anything quiet 'round yere. What's the score there then, run out of girls to date?'

'She's alright is Rosaline.'

'She's a nice girl,' said Des.

'Built for comfort I suppose,' Keg said dryly.

'She's someone I can trust. What's this I hear about Gill then, going off with Evo?'

'Aye, that tosser.'

'Did she tell you, or did you find out?'

'Just said she'd met someone else, and didn't want to see me anymore.'

'Women, ay,' Neil shrugged. 'Anyway, enjoy the rest of your night. Come on Des, let's grab a table.'

'Hey Nev,' a large well-built man, round, with a paunch, and what little hair he had was practically shaved, walked up to them. 'I 'ear your Mair wants one of those little green marble tables in David Morgan's.'

'Aye, and 'ave you seen the price on them?'

'I'll get you em, for arf the price.'

'And where are you going to get a marble table from for 'alf that price?'

'I'll put on some white overalls, go into the store, and just pick em up. No one will stop me. Think I'm one of the workies won't 'ey?'

'No, she'll go bloody mad.'

'She won't know mun.'

'She'll want to see the receipt if I give her one of those.'

'Bloody hell, who was that?' Desmond asked as they placed their drinks on an empty table, and sat down.

'Disastrous Evans. Don't buy anything off 'im.'

'I don't intend to.'

Desmond sat and watched Neil devouring a packet of crisps.

'I've got a bad feeling about all this,' there was a seriousness to Desmond's voice.

'About all what?'

'Lenny, today.'

'Aw, take no notice of that,' Neil waved a hand.

'Well, I see him sitting at a table with all the younger crowd. Youngsters are easily influenced.'

'He sits with them, as none of the mature ones want to listen to his rubbish. He's a knobhead. If he worked as much as his jaw works, he'd be a wonder.'

'I don't know, this BNP,' Desmond said slowly, shook his head and looked down into his drink, 'this BNP, it's starting to get serious.'

'If you're worrying about Bungalow 'ead and them, you're wasting your time. The organisation is a joke. A bunch of tattooed skinheads that can't string a sentence together.'

'It's not though, that's the problem. The ones taking over look like respectable businessmen in suits. They know how to talk. They can appeal to a wider crowd than Lenny and his lot.'

'Well, you'll always 'ave Wayne's lot to back you up.'

'I don't know man,' Desmond shook his head again, and gazed pensively down at the table, 'there could be riots.'

'There'll always be riots, but the police today 'ave good equipment. They'll put their water hoses on them. Aw, come on,' Neil slapped his shoulder in a friendly manner. 'Less of the long face, let's get canned.'

'Can't, I've got the car haven't I.'

'Leave it and get the train 'ome. The car will be safe in the yard. I'll go get another round in.'

Neil went to the bar and returned with a tray of two pints and two chasers.

'This will put a smile on your face,' he placed the tray on the table in front of Desmond. 'This and Amanda. 'Ow are things going with Amanda?' he asked nonchalantly.

'She's amazing,' Desmond's face relaxed, as he slouched back in the chair, and stretched his long legs out in front of him. 'I've never felt like this about a woman before. She is what is making everything bearable at the moment.'

'Careful now. You 'aven't seen her tantrums yet. I've seen her cramming fig biscuits into her gob.'

'I don't know of anything that could put me off her.'

'Where did you go last Friday, to the lack of Futures?'

'No, didn't see Amanda last Friday, as I was out on my mate's stag night.'

'That's it, of course.'

'Why, did she go out?' Desmond suddenly became attentive.

'No.'

'She told me she never went out,' Desmond looked at Neil suspiciously.

'She didn't, I remember now, Nigel came 'round.'

'She didn't tell me that,' Desmond said with slight astonishment.

'Didn't she. Well maybe she felt it unnecessary.'

'Unnecessary! To tell me she was with another man.'

'Steady on. They've known each other from kids. She's very fond of 'im. You can't expect her to drop all her friends, just because she's met you.'

'What did they do?'

'I don't know, I wasn't there all night. They were in her bedroom, when I left for the Social.'

'IN HER BEDROOM. Is she in the habit of taking men into her bedroom?'

'No, only Nigel and her female friends. You've got to understand. Her and Nigel are very close. He's the one who's been there most of her life. She tells 'im things she tells no one else.'

'How do you know?'

'She told me.'

'She tells me lots of things too.'

'Spill the beans.'

'I'm not going to grass on her to her brother. You're right,' Desmond's posture relaxed, 'she's entitled to her friendships. I just wish she'd told me that's all. Maybe she thought I'd get the wrong impression, which I did. Hell, what's the point of being with someone if you don't trust them. Come on, drink up.' Desmond sounded upbeat, but Neil noticed the concern around his mouth. An indication built from knowing someone closely for three years.

'Women ay. How we put them on a pedestal. They're all the same deep down. They're canny. They can deceive us. All sweetness and innocent smiles, while all the time, who else are they smiling at,' Neil drank the last quarter of his pint in one go, and handed the empty glass to Desmond with a wide smile.

Desmond took the glass from him, but looked at him with a quizzical expression. They continued drinking and talking, and moved on to two other pubs, before they went back to the Green Dragon. They were not in there for long, when Desmond grabbed a handful of Neil's shirt from the shoulder, and hauled him to his feet. 'Come on,' he said, 'or I'll miss the last train.'

Desmond guided Neil to the door. Neil addressed Jan the barmaid, as he was led staggering past the bar.

'I say, I say, I say, Mrs A.'

'I think you'd better get 'im out of yere before he gets a smack in the mouth,' Jan said with humour.

He managed to negotiate Neil through the door, into the lobby. They passed the fruit machine, into which a man was sacrificing handfuls of coins. He gave a shout of glee, like a child at a fairground, followed by the tinkling of a fountain of coins.

'Cor, when that air hits,' Desmond took in a deep breath, outside the pub, which opened his chest and pushed back his shoulders. Neil suddenly took off, and started running along the pavement, as if he was competing in a marathon. Desmond chased in pursuit, along the main road, which was drenched with sodium orange lamplight. The occasional car passed them, but Desmond did not recall seeing any other people. Neil slowed to a walk as Desmond caught up with him. They both walked panting alongside each other, until they reached the train platform, where they both lay on the ground, the light around them, cast from the station lamp, was a stark white. They looked up at the sky from their horizontal position, which was clear and visible due to a full moon.

'I love this place,' Desmond said, 'but why such darkness in such a beautiful place?'

'There's darkness everywhere I suppose. You just 'ave to look for the light.'

Desmond sat up in one sudden, swift movement, and twisted his head so he was looking down at Neil.

'I trust you with my life,' he said forcefully.

Neil looked at him in bewilderment, but the silence was broken by the sound of a horn, and the clatter of steel on steel. Neil half lay in a reclining position on the platform, after the train had left. After Desmond and he had stared at each other silently through the window of the train. He shook his head, stood up and wiped his palms together, before lurching out of the station to make his way home.

Chapter 14

'Thank goodness you're yere,' Amanda ran up to Desmond and gave him a hug. She noticed however his hug was not as tight and long as usual. 'I wondered if you would turn up, I've been ringing you all week.'

'Why bother ringing?' he said woodenly, 'you could have borrowed a set of drums.'

'Oh come on,' Amanda was taken aback, 'I can't 'elp it if my family think you're the wrong colour.'

'Sorry, I've just had a lot of things to do recently,' Desmond apologised unconvincingly.

'Then you can tell me all about them,' Amanda grabbed his arm, and led him past the shop windows of the high street. It was a quarter past one on a Wednesday afternoon. Desmond had agreed to work on a Saturday morning in exchange for having the afternoon off work. Amanda and he had arranged to go on another walk. Her parents had refused to have him at their house. Did they think she was going to give up so easily, Amanda had thought. That she would throw away love for something so trivial as the colour of skin. Love has no colour.

The sun was shining through muscular clouds. The kind cathedral domes tried to replicate on their ceiling murals. There were the usual steady stream of cars passing, and quite a few people milling around the high street. They were mostly women pensioners, stopping to chat on pavements, oblivious to people having to manoeuvre around them, like some obstacle course on a fun game show. The aromas were drifting out of the bakery doorway. They stopped and admired the produce on display at the window. Buns begging to be bought. Amanda went into the shop to get some baguettes and drinks for their lunch. Desmond insisted on paying, but waited outside the shop. Amanda was served by a girl chewing gum. She bought two cans of drink and two baguettes which she asked to be put in a plastic carrier bag, so it would be easy to carry, as they did not intend to be eating for at least another hour. Desmond took the bag from her when she emerged from the shop.

This time, Amanda was going to take Desmond further up the villages. He had not ventured that far, and she had been looking forward all morning to this outing. They walked along the main road for about forty-five minutes. The gaps between the traffic became longer. They turned off the main road, and once they had left the rows of terraces of the side streets, they came to a cluster of trees.

'These must be the original trees of the village,' Desmond spoke with forced lightness, 'as they are not fir trees.'

'I used to climb trees like this when I was a child.'

'You were agile then,' Desmond grinned.

'Ow about your sister. Did she climb trees?'

'Oh, it was her monkey blood,' the grin was still on his face.

Amanda also grinned and gave him a playful punch on his upper arm. Once out of the trees, the land was flat. Mountains could still be seen however, and were never out of sight, wherever one was in the villages. They passed the timber and zinc ruins of some mining edifice. A veneer of entrepreneurism which had been left behind. There was a lump of concrete in the grass, which had once probably supported a pithead bath. The air was fresh and smelt of sun heated trees and plants. There was a crackle and crunch of sunburnt grass and roots beneath their feet.

'My grandfather used to tell me the land underground yere, is honeycombed with tunnels and shafts,' Amanda said dreamily. 'This was once farming land, but farmers deserted for the coal industry.'

'And now the coal industry has deserted them,' Desmond replied solemnly.

'Sad innit?'

'Not really. The land is green and beautiful now, not marred by black gouges. The air is clean, and not stained with soot.'

'There are no jobs though, that's the problem.'

'Not in mining no. Something needs to replace that. Why not farm again?'

'No money in it.'

'Better than being on benefits.'

'Ard work, long hours, competition from other countries.'

'Make Aedre a brand. Someone could start an ice cream factory, play on the fresh air and mountains as advertising.'

'I don't know. You'll 'ave to speak to Wayne about that. He talks about incentives given to encourage employers to set up industry yere, but some fail and others relocate to cheaper labour. He was outside some factory gate yere protesting against closure the other week. The owner who took over Wayne said, was not committed to the villages. Decay is becoming exponential he said, or some such thing. "You can see it all around in fallen factories."

'What on earth is that?' Desmond pointed to a row of derelict houses, full of skylight and glassless window holes. Apart from the house on the end with a roof, and wispy smoke coming out of the chimney, and a tin bath hanging on the wall. 'That looks odd, out here.'

'That's Mr Wilbermot. He refused to leave when the street was demolished.'

'What does he do for water and electricity?

'Candles and water from the stream.'

'There are people living like that in remote villages in Africa, and are given aid by charities such as Oxfam.'

The land yawning all around them looked too big for the house. They walked further where the grass became greener and started to rise to the swelling mountain. Some sheep nibbled grass. A man and woman came sauntering from the opposite direction, and acknowledged them as they passed.

'Out here in this wilderness, and you see someone you know!' Desmond said in disbelief.

'Friends are made in a matter of days yere.'

They passed sheep, which were chest deep in grass, as they ascended the slope. There was the aroma of grass being cooked by the sun.

'Let's stop yere and 'ave dinner,' Amanda said through quick breaths.

'It's a nice spot,' Desmond nodded, 'great view from here. I should have brought something to sit on. I didn't bring a jacket, I thought it was too warm.'

'Of course it is, you would be sweltering, although, remember that park in Casteldaeg, on that really 'ot day, and there were those women in thick knitted cardigans.'

'They looked Somalian, so they were from a hot country mind. What is hot to you, may be cold to them.'

'Ow on earth do they manage in winter then?' Amanda felt the grass. 'The ground is not wet, and it's not dirty either, so we can sit on the grass, it's ok.'

They sat there quietly, the click and hiss of their cans being opened was the only sound. Desmond looked at the rows of streets clinging to the mountain opposite, as if trying to fathom it out. The land gave grass to the grazing sheep, those nomads of the mountains. Yet those same mountains crushed those who picked at their innards. Those who were driven by greedy entrepreneurs after the black riches. 'It's like entering a new world here,' he said distantly, 'it even has its own climate. You know, some days I can leave Casteldaeg and its fine, yet as soon as I get past Briog it starts to rain. Strangers are looked upon with suspicion. There is an oppressive stillness to the place.'

'Behind the times you mean.'

'There's no dinosaurs here, but I'm looked at as if I've crawled from prehistory.'

'Black people 'aven't reached this far yet. You are unique,' Amanda grabbed his arm and pulled him close to her.

'Yeah, but not in a nice way,' Desmond said sullenly.

'You are to me.'

'I mean your parents.' There was a slight exasperation to his tone, and his face tightened. 'I've been polite to them, treated them with respect, treated you well, yet they look on me as some kind of uncivilised savage.'

'Oh, not as bad as that.'

'Well, I can match them on any scale,' Desmond asserted. 'I'll show them what kind of man I am.'

'It makes no difference,' Amanda shook her head sadly. 'You could be St Paul for all they care. Unless you can change the colour of your skin, and you're not a chameleon.'

Amanda used the corner of her serviette to wipe the remains of barbecue sauce from the sides of her mouth.

'Tiggy's not like that,' she said.

'Who?'

'Nigel.'

'Tiggy,' Desmond almost spat the name out with distaste. 'So that's what you call him is it?'

'I was saying to 'im the other night.'

'Oh, will you stop talking about him,' Desmond burst out angrily, and shot straight up onto his feet. 'Nigel, Nigel, Nigel. That skinny little wimp, that's all I seem to hear.' He picked up his half-empty can and hurled it into the distance, with the force of a shot putter.

Amanda's mouth fell open, and she stared at Desmond, as she frantically struggled to find words.

'Sorry,' her voice was quiet and shaking, 'I didn't realise I spoke about 'im that often. It's just, we've been friends for years. That's all we've ever been, and ever can be,' Amanda said bewildered. 'We're like brother and sister. The thought of anything else, would seem wrong to both of us.'

A heavy melancholy brooded over the next forty-five minutes. They spoke little, and Desmond's jaw seemed clenched throughout. Amanda wondered whether her words had been enough. The silence enlarged; unspoken words hung in the air. Amanda tried to disguise the relief she felt when Desmond said moodily, 'we'd better get going. We don't know how much longer this sun is going to last.'

They walked back in silence mostly. The air was thick with unease. An awkwardness so thick, it was difficult to ignore. A gloom seemed to had settled upon them.

Chapter 15

Neil held open the door of the Social for Rosaline. He was wearing his best dark green sweater, which he kept for special occasions, and had got Amanda to press his jeans, so there was a sharp, knife-edge crease down the front. He had polished his brown, size nine brogues before leaving the house. Rosaline was wearing a cream blouse, with a floral print, and black trousers, which made her look slimmer than she actually was. The sides of her feet however, bulged over her one-inch heel, sling-back shoes.

Being a Wednesday evening, there were quite a few empty tables. Neil caught sight of Wayne by the bar.

'Are we just in time?' Neil raised his eyebrows quizzically, a hint of a smile around his mouth.

'Too late, I've just paid. Getting one for the Guvnor ain't I.'

'How about your brother then?'

'Tell you what, Don,' Wayne shouted to the bartender, who was serving someone else, 'put these two on my tab,' he inclined his head towards Neil and Rosaline. 'I'll pay for them on my next round.' Don gave a nod of his head.

'How's things Ros?' Wayne addressed Rosaline.

'Fine, thanks, and you?'

'Can't complain.'

'Well, you're an 'appily settled man now.'

'Under the thumb,' Neil joked, pointing the thumb of his closed fist to the floor.

'Oh don't listen to 'im,' Rosaline said, 'you've got a good one in Anita my Mam says.'

'She keeps me on the straight and narrow.'

'You were never off the straight and narrow,' Neil quipped, 'any spare seats around by you?'

'Yeah, come and sit with us.'

They picked up their drinks and followed Wayne to a table in the right-hand corner of the room, where three men were already seated. Two were sitting on a long, high backed, plush velvet seat against the wall. Two were in their late fifties, and one in his early seventies. The latter had leathery skin, which creased around his neck, accordion style. His head was small, it emerged between the collars of his white shirt like a tortoise. His pale blue eyes however, had an inclination to laughter.

'All right Guvnor,' Wayne handed a full pint glass to the man in his seventies.

'Jimbo, Dai?' Neil nodded towards the Guvnor and the other two men in the high-backed seat, who returned the nod. 'This is Rosaline, tonight's special guest.'

'Ello,' Rosaline said chirpily.

'He's a mean sod, bringing you yere. He should 'ave taken you somewhere nicer,' said the man who had been addressed as Jimbo.

'This is nice,' Rosaline said brightly. 'Nice people, nice drinks, what more can I want?'

'Aye, you get a tidy pint yere, fair play,' said the other man, Dai.

'He's a good lad, is Wayne,' said Guvnor, 'always buys me a pint.'

'Not for much longer,' said Jimbo, 'his money will be going on carpets and cutlery soon.'

'Ah, I'm sure I'll find some spare to buy Guvnor a drink.'

'Early finish for you on Wednesday is it?' Neil started a conversation with Rosaline, while the other men conversed amongst themselves. Dai spoke little, but listened to the male conversation, and smiled at Rosaline now and again.

'Alternate Wednesdays,' she replied.

'Not like Amanda then, she doesn't work Wednesdays, and the salon closes 'alf day.'

'No such luck for me.'

'Do you meet up with Amanda on Wednesdays?'

'Sometimes, but not so much since she met Des. In fact, not much at all now. Although I do get the impression that things are not as good with Des now.'

'Yeah,' Neil turned his full attention on Rosaline, 'in what way?'

'Well, she used to be all gushing, when she first started seeing Desmond. Talked about 'im all the time, and she always looked so 'appy. But she's been looking down lately, and when I ask about Desmond, she just shrugs, and says, "he's changed."'

'In what way?' Neil leant a little closer towards her.

'I don't know.'

'Does she ever say anything?'

'Well, not so much to me. She says he's quieter now, and moody. She 'as to be careful what she says to 'im.'

'Really! What on earth could that be?'

'Like, the other day, she mentioned Nigel, and he went right off on one.'

Neil looked intrigued, 'Why, what did he say?'

'Well, I didn't like to press, and she changed the subject.'

'Maybe she needs someone to talk to. Why don't you tell her you're concerned about her, give her a chance to get things off her chest?'

'Well, she may tell Nigel more.'

'Do you think?'

'She's been seeing 'im more, recently.' Neil gave her an encouraging look, 'He's the one she seems to turn to, when things go wrong.'

'Does she?' Neil sat back in his chair with a smug look.

'Oh yeah, loads of people think there is something between 'em. Think they will end up married. She laughs when I tell her. "I can't imagine Nigel as anything other than a friend," she says. "We know too much about each other, seen all our habits, 'ow many sherbet lemons we can cram into our mouths."'

Neil tilted his head back and laughed. He listened intently as Rosaline continued talking, he laughed and nodded at certain points.

'I went on a few demonstrations,' Jimbo was saying to Wayne, Guvnor and Dai, who just nodded silently. 'Our boys were no angels, but the police,' he shook his head.

'I was on the front line at one,' said Guvnor, 'I went right up to this young copper, I held my stick under his nose. He pushed me back into the strikers, who caught me and said, "Yes, you lay a finger on him, butt." I went back up to the copper, and said, "I think it's disgusting what you're doing to these men. I fought in the last war, and I've *killed* better men than you."'

'That was Thatcher won't it,' Wayne said scathingly, 'all her talk of bringing harmony to discord.'

'Huh,' said Dai.

'Bloody Thatcher,' murmured Jimbo.

'Police intimidation and harassment, it was a violation of people's rights. Democracy,' Wayne said bitterly, 'police whacking unarmed miners with truncheons. Men who were only dressed in jeans and tee shirts. Chasing them on horseback. It was a fascist regime.'

'And the press blamed us,' said Jimbo. 'What did they expect? Yeah, we threw whatever we could get our 'ands on, in defence. We didn't go there armed with batons. And looks what's 'appening now? Aedre is losing its purpose. Steelworks closed, mines closed, what next? It'll be the clothes factory next. You mark my words. Jeff's boy 'ad to speak to some jumped up official at the dole office the other day. "What can I do?" he asked. "Try Manchester," they said. Bloody Manchester, there should be jobs yere for them.'

'That's our cue to go,' Neil stood up.

'Where you off now?' asked Jimbo.

'The Falstaff.'

'The Futures, not that youth club,' Jimbo said sarcastically, 'anyone over eighteen there is old.'

'The young lady will be alright,' said Guvnor, 'you'd better not go there,' he said to Wayne.

'I bloody well won't, don't you worry.'

'A man's pub you want,' said Jimbo, 'not that bloody Mickey Mouse effort.'

'Well, it's been lovely to 'ave met you all,' Rosaline said cheerily.

'And you too,' said Guvnor. 'I would 'ave liked to 'ave spoken with you more, only this one,' he pointed at Neil, 'as been keeping you to 'iself all night.'

'I don't want any of you lot trying to take her away from me,' said Neil.

'Aw, well, maybe we'll 'ave a catch-up next time,' said Rosaline, 'and I'll buy you a drink.'

'The ladies don't buy drinks with us,' Guvnor replied.

'I'll be drunk then, with you lot all buying me drinks,' Rosaline laughed.

The light had turned to darkness when they got outside the Social. It was cool, but not cold, and the sky overhead was full of stars. A sweet, yeasty aroma seeped from the opened windows of the Social.

'The Futures then,' Neil said, whilst zipping up his light sports jacket.

They could see more of the décor of the Futures on a Wednesday than they could on a Friday and Saturday. There were worn patches on the cranberry-coloured carpet, apart from which, the rest of the place did not look too bad. The landlord gave the walls a coat of cream paint every year, and the woven tapestry effect of the seating, was quite hard wearing.

'There's Sharon over there,' Neil nodded towards three girls sitting near the wall. 'Why don't you go and join her, I'll come over in a bit with the drinks.'

Rosaline greeted the girls, who invited her and Neil to join them.

Nigel was sitting with a group of young men two tables over, and was in a conversation with the one sitting next to him.

'I'm getting a bit fed up with this Tig. Beer, piss and fag outside. There's gotta be more to life than this mun.'

'I know what you mean Jacks. We need to find ourselves a woman.'

'And what little money you 'ave, goes to them. No thanks.'

'So it's giving our money to the brewery instead then.'

'I'm in at six tomorrow, to pack pissing sliced bread on racks. Can't even 'ave a fag outside now, without the floor fascist coming out.'

'Same yere butt. We used to 'ave a laugh. Can't do anything now without the anti-fun fascists coming round. "Elf and safety innit mate". Some woman shopped Matty the other day for harassment. All he did was say "'Ello luv."'

'I worked to get my GCSEs. What's the bloody point? And one of the Guys has an A-level! "Well, you get life skills working on the shop floor," says floor fascist. Life skills in what? Stacking bloody jars of mayo! I was speaking to Brits the other week. Came 'ome from the army. Travelling the world, money in his pocket. Tells me about all the girls he 'as. Is like the whole world is a success, and I'm turning into a sad fat sack.'

'So *he* says' Nigel said doubtfully. 'Is that that all you want Jacks? He's not exactly learning a trade. He'll be out in six years, back yere, where all his friends are married or moved on. I've seen it all before. Seen them, hanging onto the glory of tours in Ireland or the Falklands. Look at Mad Mike, he's a bloody wreck. My mother saw 'im once on a train, in his uniform, must 'ave been coming 'ome on leave. He was staggering about as drunk as a skunk. Somebody asked 'im which stop he was getting off on. A blokey put 'im out at his stop, and said to the passengers, "That's what Northern Ireland does to you." It doesn't mean anything.'

'Yeah, like all of us by yuh now, tonight, tomorrow night and Friday night. Look at Neil now. The women he's 'ad, and now he's resorted to Rosaline.'

'Well maybe he's realised, like us, that there's more to life. Rosaline's a nice girl. She wouldn't pass you by on the road without saying 'ello. Not like some, and the set who went away to uni,' Nigel tilted his head back slightly and rolled his eyes. 'Remember Laura? She used to be a really nice girl. Saw her back Christmas time. Walked straight past me. Who does she think she is ay? Her mother is a dinner lady, and her father is a postman.'

'All these high ideas you get when drunk. You've got it all worked out. Of 'ow you will change your life. Go to college, get a trade. Then you wake up in the morning. With a kick in the ass hangover, and realise it's all an illusion. You ain't going anywhere. You open the curtains, and there is Aedre.'

'Take a trip on the road to nowhere. Why don't you do something Jacks? Going to college is not a bad idea.'

'Yeah, and there's about ten of us chasing one job when we finish. All the Poles coming over now, taking the jobs. Can't give up what piss-poor job I 'ave. As I won't get another.'

Neil returned from the bar, 'All right girls,' he handed Rosaline a drink.

'You took your time,' one of the girls said. 'Not exactly crowded at the bar is it?'

'Got talking to Dai Stripes didn't I.'

'These men, they're worse than the women when it comes to gassing.'

'Well I won't disturb your conversation then. I'll come back later.'

'Something we said?' asked one of the girls.

'Naw, it's just Nigel's over there, and I want to 'ave a catch up with 'im.'

'Yeah, you want to talk man things, like sport,' said one of the girls. 'We know, we won't be offended.'

'They want to talk about women mun,' said the other girl, at which all four girls guffawed.

'Right, that's it,' said Neil, 'I'm going off in disgust now,' Neil was glad of an excuse to get away from the fast, gossipy energy.

Neil took a seat next to Nigel, who although sitting with four other guys, no longer seemed to be that involved in the conversation with the guy sitting next to him.

'Hey Nev,' said one of the guys, 'ow's things going?'

'Alright, 'ow are things with you Potts?'

'No complaints, this isn't your usual haunt.'

'On a date ain't I. Got to take her somewhere 'alf decent.'

'Aye, I hear you're with Rosaline now. What 'appened, ran out of girls to date?'

'Looking for some personality. What about you, I don't exactly see women queuing at your door,' Neil said sourly.

'Staying single, best way. No woman telling me what to do.'

'Not an excuse for something else is it?' Neil gave a mischievous grin.

'I'm sensible.'

'Yeah, more like women aren't interested in 'im,' said the other guy.

'You look like you've seen 'appier days,' Neil said to Nigel, whilst the other four guys went back into conversation.

'Yeah, well it's not exactly swinging yere is it?'

'Not got a girlfriend yet then?'

'No.'

'Are you looking for one?'

Rosaline and her friends could be heard guffawing again.

'They've been like that all night.'

'Yeah, I thought I would leave them to it. Anyway, I'll 'ave a better laugh talking with men. So, are you looking for a girlfriend?'

'Aren't we all?'

'Anyone special, you 'ave your eye on.'

'No, not much choice around yere.'

'I've got a sister who lives yere you know,' Neil pretended to be offended.

'Oh, I don't mean her,' Nigel said quickly, 'Amanda, I mean. Amanda is out of bounds really.'

'Why's that?'

'We've been friends for years. Never really considered us as being anything other than friends. Besides, she's in love with Desmond.'

'Are you sure?'

'Well, things aren't exactly buzzing between them at the moment, but I dare say it will pass.'

'She's not 'appy, and I'm worried about her.'

'I don't know what's wrong with 'im. The guy's an idiot. He had an ep last week, over nothing!'

'We both care about her, don't we?'

'Yeah,' Nigel nodded solemnly.

'She likes you, you know.'

'I know, but as a friend.'

'No, it's more than that.'

'What makes you say that?' Nigel sat up straight suddenly, looking at Neil with wide eyes.

'The way she talks about you, the way she looks at you. Believe me I know women,' Neil winked, stood up, and walked back over to Rosaline and her friends.

Chapter 16

Amanda walked past a trio of elderly ladies, who were sat on a bench at the grassy space, between where the terraced streets ended and the mountainside began. How concerned they seemed to be on the vagaries of illness and the weather. A silence fell as Amanda approached. She smiled at them, a smile which they returned, but she was aware she would probably be the next subject of their conversation. She had learnt to ignore the critical glances, reluctant smiles and sideways looks, just as she had learnt to ignore the frequent rain. Last night she had been awoken, by one of those sounds that is an attempt to scream by the dreamer. She must have tossed and turned for about an hour, and the next noise to raise her from sleep, was the alarm clock piercing the morning silence. It was Wednesday morning, there was no need for the alarm clock to have gone off that morning. She must have forgotten to switch it off the previous evening. She nevertheless decided to get up, have some breakfast, go for a walk, so she would not have to spend much time around the house when her mother arose.

She wondered how things could have turned so different in such a short space of time. Why, just two months ago, she was planning her marriage. It was a white, sterile day, with no blue in the sky. There was a smell of damp leaves. She stopped halfway up the mountain, where she was still within sight of the houses below, but the sounds of the street were distant, the faint sounds of car horns or bark of a dog. Desmond was never far from her mind, but she thought of how quickly the sweetness had turned so sour. That morning, she had looked through photographs of them together, pictures of smiles long since left behind. How she wished time had stopped at that point. She longed for his doting brown eyes, those small physical gestures, like the way he touched her chin with the backs of his fingers, which affirmed his strength of feeling for her. Being in love felt not having to explain it. Now, he was always morose, her attempts to communicate with him only seemed to agitate him further. Yet, she could not envision a future without him.

Amanda noticed groups of mushrooms around a tree, that looked like carbuncles growing out of its roots. She surveyed the dull brown streets below, through a haze of thick gloom. What was it about this place that now seemed so lacklustre? What had only a few months ago been so glittering and exciting, was now dimmed. Why did love have to hurt so much, she thought. The movies made out it was a burst of sunshine. The heart should be soaring with ecstasy. She listened to a bird repeating itself, the same song, over and over. Was it a love song? Had this thrush's or blackbird's heart been broken? Are these birds listening to my thoughts? Can they hear what I think?

'Are you? You black feathered sons of bitches,' she addressed some crows perched on a nearby fence. 'Are you mocking me?'

The birds made insolent noises back at her.

Amanda caught sight of the church steeple, like a finger pointing to heaven. There aren't any buildings like that today, she thought. We haven't really progressed. Look at all the beautiful medieval churches and cathedrals still standing solidly. Would her love last, like the churches? All the technology we have today, and what have we produced?

She and Desmond had something special. She was not going to let that be taken from her. They had something worth fighting for, and she was going to fight for it.

'I 'ave decided,' she shouted to the backs of household gardens, and her decision was like a released spring, scattering tension over rooftops. I have decided, her feet said to the grass, as she strode down the sloping ground, energy strengthening every muscle of her body. She walked triumphantly back through the streets of terraced houses, where morning lives were commencing. Curtains were being opened; milk bottles were being picked up from door steps. She stopped outside the cinema, and found herself staring at a billboard on the side of its wall. The billboard was advertising some range of car.

'I didn't ask to fall in love,' she shouted at the billboard.

Some passers-by gave her strange looks, but she didn't care, she continued walking, arms swinging, and looked directly into the eyes of people she passed. She was proceeding to the church, which was her intended target, since it came into sight from the mountain. She did not want to go back to the house, and face her father's sullen mood, and mother's moans, even though she felt as if nothing could dampen her present state of mind. She did not want to risk damage to the joy she currently felt.

Amanda entered the huge, yawning silence of the church, and sat on one of the hard, wooden benches. The air smelt cool and musty, that mothball smell of musty old book or antique shops. She admired the multi-coloured light, streaming through the stained-glass windows. She had not been in the church for some time. The last time was on a Christmas Eve with Sharon, Melissa and some others, after an evening spent in the Futures. They had caused a disturbance with their talking and giggling. The vicar stopped the service at one point and glared at them. When Melissa told him to carry on, well, Amanda had been so embarrassed, she had not been into the church since.

'Amanda Williams, well this is indeed a pleasant surprise.' Amanda turned to see the vicar walking down the aisle. 'What brings you here today?' he smiled broadly and took a seat in front of her. Gerwyn, the vicar, was in his early thirties, and had lived in the villages all his life, apart from when he left to study for the ministry. He was dressed today in his black cassock, and white collar. He had a youthfulness to him, and a pleasant manner. He was popular with many in the villages, and not just the church going community.

'I was passing, and as I 'adn't been in yere for a long time, I thought I would call in.'

'And I'm glad you did,' the vicar said cheerfully. 'Something tells me however, you are not happy,' he said in a more serious voice.

Amanda told him of Desmond, and the opposition to their relationship.

'They see his colour as ugly,' Amanda said sadly. 'Why can't they see how beautiful it is?' she gently fingered the pink stone of her pendant.

'He is a victim of white judgement. Beauty comes from the inside. Jesus after all was not pale skinned and blue eyed. He would have been pretty conspicuous walking around Galilee had he been.' Amanda gave a confused look. 'Oh, you didn't think he was white, did you?' the vicar asked. 'That was how he was portrayed. God too was shown as pale, male and stale. Why would God have needed a beard, and why was he bald?! I mean most men suffering with alopecia would have loved hair. If you were the creator of the world, and could do anything you wanted, would you make yourself bald?!' he looked at Amanda, a smile playing around his lips.

'My uncle is bald,' Amanda laughed, 'and he would love to 'ave hair. Any colour, even ginger.'

'Exactly,' the vicar smiled, 'images we have been given of the almighty, are man's constructs. White is associated with goodness and purity. Black with negativity. Look at how sin is portrayed, black magic, prince of darkness. Vampires only come out under the shadow of darkness.' He holds out his arms, forming his cassock into wings, placing the top layer of his teeth over his bottom lip, causing Amanda to laugh even more.

'I sometimes think God is a pretty mean guy,' she turned melancholy again. 'I mean, if you were to create the world, would you create cancer?'

'Oh, God's creation is wonderful,' the vicar enthused. 'Everything in nature is so fine tuned. I'm sure there is even a reason for such a horrid disease to exist.'

'Most wars are fought over religion?'

'God does not decide wars, man does.'

'Why didn't God create people as kind, not aggressive?'

'Because God gave free will, and it is a wonderful gift. Without it, we would just be robots,' the vicar smiled benignly at Amanda. 'We need to shed some light in the darkness. It should not be all negativity. There is much good in the world, but it is often engulfed by all the bad things that happen, until it is difficult to see the goodness. The problem is, it's everywhere, and people are becoming immune to it. One moment the news is showing people being shot in a war zone, the next, there is a shootout in some detective series. This blurs the line between fantasy and reality.'

Amanda nodded silently.

'When I was a child,' the vicar continued. 'I had pistols, bows and arrows. There were war films and westerns on the tv. Why this assumption that boys want to fight? Why not teach them love and compassion?'

'Where is the motivation in forgiveness?' Amanda murmured.

'Motivation is to be kind. Make the world a better place. Humans are more alike than unalike. What it all boils down to, is we all want the same. We all want to be safe, and for our children to grow up in a safe world. If only everyone could realise that. I have seen hatred amongst the hearts of men in this community. This community which prides itself on its hospitality.'

Amanda looked at him curiously.

'We have seen dark times here,' the vicar said morosely. 'During the miner's strike, a taxi driver, not part of the cause at all, was killed, whilst taking miners to work.'

'On purpose?' Amanda said with shock.

'Oh no, no. It was manslaughter. It wasn't the intention for anyone to get killed that day. He was the innocent victim of a conflict which pitted neighbour against neighbour. Why does it take the death of a man to realise what hatred leads to?' The vicar shook his head sadly. 'Yes, the history of the coalface has been one of oppression and ruined rivers.'

'Wayne says, if it were not for coal there would 'ave been no iron or steel. There would 'ave been no civilisation.'

'Are we really civilised?' the vicar raised his eyebrows quizzically. 'I often think of the early American settlers. The

Pilgrim Fathers, hitched up in the *Mayflower*, when it took anchor. Could they have envisioned the capitalism, slavery and oppression that was to ensue? The Native Americans of course, are now seen as correct. Their philosophy on the environment. Well, we are where we are,' the vicar said resignedly, 'and now controls need to be put in place. We now know the catastrophic effects of pollution. We can no longer just close our eyes. Anyway,' the vicar's voice became lighter, 'I don't want you leaving here all depressed. I remember when I was in the choir here, and you were a child. You would all chant something about the vicar.

'Yes,' Amanda said a little embarrassed, but amused, 'we used to call 'im the Parson, after a Parson in a children's story.'

They both lifted their chins and laughed.

'We called 'im the Parson,' Amanda sang, 'because of the size of his no...oo...oo...ose.' She then talked wistfully, of how she loved coming to church at Christmas, of seeing the nativity figures. 'There was Jesus in the crib,' she reminisced, 'a donkey, cows and the three wise men.'

'Ah yes, the three wise men. One was black. I believe it was meant to show we are all equal before God. And who can dispute God's word. Racism is a social construct,' the vicar said sadly. 'I'm afraid the world is run by men who think they are right.'

'And women?' Amanda said with a sardonic smile.

'Yes, and women,' the vicar smiled back. 'Have you read *Heart of Darkness* by Joseph Conrad?'

Amanda shook her head.

'The film *Apocalypse Now* is based on it.'

'Oh, Wayne loves that film,' Amanda said effusively. 'He's seen it about twenty times. "Exterminate with extreme prejudice,"' Amanda quoted in a low, grim voice. 'It was about a journey up a river.' Amanda put on an uncomprehending expression.

'Conrad was impressed by Livingstone. Livingstone was a missionary. The aim of the missionaries was to bring light to those who had not heard the Lord's word. But he was ruthless and entrepreneurial, and a team was sent into Africa to find him. *Heart of Darkness* was not a story of white triumphalism, but what happens to Europeans when they become embroiled in other cultures.'

The vicar took a breath before continuing. 'Conrad was devastated by what Leopold was doing to natives in the Congo.'

'Leopold?'

'He was the King of Belgium, who laid claim to the Congo. The character Kurtz in the novel was probably Leopold. Subjugating the natives with brutality and torture, to gain ivory. Kurtz used possessive language, "My ivory, My intended." It was about a man having too much power, overreaching himself. Conrad could not talk of his experiences in the Congo for years. The journey up the river, may have been a journey into hell. Marlowe looked into the abyss, but stepped back. Kurtz was a very accomplished character, who could have been a musician in the Western world, but becomes a savage. Something changed in him in the wilderness. He wrote a report, which started out very lofty, with high ideals, but got worse, ending with "Exterminate the Brutes."'

Amanda's eyes widened, but she remained silent and expectant.

'There was much discussion in the eighteenth century you see. Darwinism talked of evolution as progress, but it was wondered whether it was possible for people to degenerate, go backwards. *Heart of Darkness* raises the question, who were the real savages? Kurtz's last words "The horror, the horror," succinct, yet says so much. Something unnameable, can mean different things to different people. It is uncomfortable reading alright. Anyway, do you remember that Christmas Eve you disrupted my service?' the vicar said teasingly.

Amanda covered her smile with her hand.

'You were very drunk,' the vicar pointed playfully at her.

'I didn't want to get out of bed the next morning. Couldn't believe what we'd done.'

'I expect you had quite a headache,' the vicar grinned.

'Not really, I was used to it in those days.'

'Here comes the organist, to tune the organ.'

'I'd better get going,' Amanda stood up, and made her way to the door, accompanied by the vicar.

'Thank you so much vicar,' Amanda stopped at the door, 'that talk with you, 'as made me feel so much better.'

'I hope the next time I see you in church will be before your wedding,' the vicar gave her a knowing look.

'I don't know when that will be.'

'Think hard before you decide. Young love can be very arrogant and delusional. I marry many, and see them when the moment is years behind them, and they are no longer together,' he said sorrowfully.

'My father probably won't be at my wedding,' Amanda said unhappily.

The vicar put a hand on the back of her shoulder, 'One day, they will be sorry about what they have started,' he said mildly.

Chapter 17

'It's a dumping ground for problem families,' Sheila, a social worker said flatly.

'That's what a lot of people say,' Amanda replied passively, whilst filing Sheila's nails. She was one of Amanda's many regulars. A woman in her early forties, with short, dyed light brown hair. Probably dyed to cover up the grey, which would be an inevitable consequence of her vocation. Her face had settled into that drab tone of resignation.

'It's as if they have a right to fail,' her voice was raised slightly, with frustration. 'Mind you, not much thought went into the scheme. It was designed by unimaginative planners.'

'I suppose,' Amanda sounded absentminded. Sheila's voice sounded as if it was coming from somewhere remote and far away.

'As soon the grass is dry, it will be set alight. Why set fire to it for fun? To see the little green you have, go up in smoke. Leaving unattractive burnt patches. Everything else in Brynhalig is so ugly, they think why not, I suppose.'

Amanda drifted off into a reverie, whilst the voice opposite her became like a slow moving river. A meandering monotone, flowing to midday, which would be her next customer. The last before lunchbreak, when she would meet Nigel.

'He says he never felt he'd left the army,' Sheila's voice came back into Amanda's mind. 'I'm not surprised, I thought, living here. The place is like an army barracks. "Of course," he says, "the women couldn't get their knickers off quick enough."'

Amanda smiled weakly.

'"Did you kill anyone out there?" the woman's voice increased two octaves, in mocking imitation of the women speaking to the soldier. '"Loads love, loads,"' her voice decreased to imitate that of the soldier. '"Only none of them Argies. The military is like a family," he says, "well it is until you're out, then you're on your own." "I don't understand that," his wife says, "Well bloody well try," he snaps.'

'Sad,' Amanda said sympathetically, 'ow long 'as he been married?'

'About three years. They have a one-year-old.'

'I suppose he was 'oping marriage would 'elp 'im put it all behind 'im.' Amanda said, with no genuine interest.

'It doesn't though. He still has bad dreams. Wakes up in the god forsaken hours. He drinks to forget.'

'Poor bloke, and the poor wife and child. I was only a child myself when all that was 'appening, but Anita said she cried when it came on the news a ship had been sunk.'

'HMS *Sheffield*, I expect.'

'I can remember seeing a picture on the front of the newspaper, of a ship type thing, on the sea, and Wayne saying, "Can't believe Britain is at war." And the news, all these people cheering, and the camera fixed on this one older woman, and my mother going, "Oh shut up, you silly cow. You've lost anyway."'

'There is a lot of drinking problems going on. Getting them to the AA is the challenge. First of all, they have to admit they have a problem. I called around to one of my regulars the other day. "Good morning," he says to me. "I'm worried about you," I say. "Why are you worried about me," he asks. "Well it is not morning, for one thing," I say, "it is two o'clock in the afternoon,"' at which Amanda shakes her head, with a slight smile. 'He probably feels great after a drink,' Sheila continued. 'He no doubt thinks, yeah, I've had a drink, so what? He can't see he is staggering along the street. Then, they have to want to change. I can understand why some of them drink. Blimey, if I had five kids all under the age of eleven, I probably would. They drink to blot out the pain and loneliness. It's breaking that circle. The AA gives them that support network.'

'Good there is something like that. Any road, 'ow is Gemma getting along in her new job?' Amanda tried to sound interested.

'Oh fine, but she doesn't know whether she wants to do it all her life. Said it's boring. She's talking about going into nursing.'

'Well, that's a worthwhile job.' Amanda was relying on her subconscious to provide replies.

'It is, well, there's no future in retail.'

'And Paul. 'Appily plumbing his way through life?'

'Yes, he's seems to like it, talking about running his own business at some stage. "It's hard bloody slog," Derek tells him.'

'I guess people will always need plumbers.'

'You're right there. One of his friends is self-employed, and always boasting about how little tax he pays. Being his own boss, and all that, answerable to nobody. Yes, I say, and if the Revenue get wind of it, he'll have a right mega tax bill landing on his doorstep. I've a good mind to ring the Revenue myself.'

'There you go Sheila. Nails looking lovely,' Amanda stood up, waited while Sheila examined her nails, and followed her to the counter.

After dealing with Sheila's payment, and saying their goodbyes, Amanda tidied her work table, and sat down to await her next client. She watched the passing show of street life outside. A steady stream of traffic. Sometimes a driver would wind down the window, to shout to some passer-by he knew. People going in and out of shops. Some to only one or two shops, others strolling past, looking in most shop windows, and stopping to talk with others on the pavement. A man in his fifties was standing on the corner, with a cigarette held between his thumb and forefinger. He had that familiar paunchy shape of men past their prime. His head still had a few strands of hair, which men losing their hair try to cling to. 'Awright Cyril?' another man, a few years younger said, on passing him. 'Yeah, 'ow's things with you Stu?' the older man replied. 'Yeah fine,' the younger man shouted back. 'And the missus?' 'Yeah, she's fine too.'

Amanda thought of Desmond, who was her escape from this drudgery. She didn't know what was happening there though, at the moment. Their passion had turned to a dull ache, although she still longed for him. The only equation she knew was him and her, but he was becoming distant. Conversation which had once flowed so freely between them was now an effort. She had sensed the tremors for the past few weeks now. His questioning over Nigel. Neil had mentioned she was fond of Nigel. 'Why did you 'ave to say that?' she accused Neil. 'You 'ave caused me trouble.' 'I didn't mean to, it just kind of slipped out,' Neil had said, raising his palms to the ceiling in exasperation. 'I told 'im you were just friends, that's all. You can 'ave friends.' 'No, I'm not dropping it,' Desmond had said to her angrily, the blackness of his dilated pupils, holding her to the wall, 'not until you tell me what Neil meant.'

Yes, she had admitted she liked Nigel, and yes, she spent time with him as a friend. She could not help what people said, she had tried to reason. The silence was worse than the arguing. His smile, now disappeared as quickly as it appeared, and it did not appear that often.

Amanda's thoughts stopped abruptly at the sound of a gush of air through the opened door.

'Good morning Mrs Richards,' Amanda cheerily greeted, along with her other two co-workers.

Mrs Richards, a woman in her late sixties, with drawn on eyebrows, and maroon lipstick stains on her teeth, looked down at her watch, and smiled the width of her wire rimmed glasses.

'Well, it's just about morning,' she said in a low voice, neither loud, nor quiet, but with a clear resonance.

'Take a seat,' Amanda indicated the chair in front of her. 'Your usual shade of pink?'

'Yes, my usual please.' Mrs Richards placed her palms flat on the table before her. Her fingers, chunky with gold rings, were splayed like starfish.

Amanda's nostrils twitched slightly, at the overpowering pungency of perfume. Later in the day, the strong aroma of perfume and chocolate would permeate the workspace. Her brothers could not stay in the salon too long, otherwise they would succumb to nausea.

'And 'ow are we today then?' Amanda asked chirpily.

'Very well thank you, and yourself?'

'Fine,' Amanda emphasised the word fine, 'and 'ow is Bertie?'

'Oh, he's good. I took him out for his walk this morning, see. I will need to call into the pet shop on the way back, as I've run out of his favourite biscuits.'

'Oh well, we can't 'ave that can we?'

'No, he won't be happy, if I don't get them.'

Amanda spent the next fifteen minutes, carefully stroking varnish onto her client's nails. 'There you go, just place under the drier now, and you will be all set for another fortnight.'

Mrs Richards seemed to be straining under a great weight as she got up from her seat, as if clambering out of a collapsed building. Having to take great care, to manoeuvre around hanging steel girders and piles of rubble.

'You ladies look after yourselves now,' Mrs Richards said to Amanda and her colleagues, 'and I'll see you in two weeks.'

'We look forward to that,' Amanda said, 'don't forget Bertie's biscuits now.'

'She goes with another man, so what?' We all make mistakes, and she is entitled to, being a woman. The weaker sex and all that. Do you think you're the only man to 'ave fallen for the wrong woman?' Neil was walking beside Desmond. He had suggested going to the high street delicatessen to get some lunch. You need cheering up, he had told Desmond.

'She assures me she hasn't,' Desmond said anxiously, 'and I want to believe her.'

'Well then,' Neil shrugged.

'I don't know,' Desmond said uncertainly, looking up into the distance.

'Exactly, you don't know, therefore, it could be all in your mind.'

'Yet, you've said they like each other, and have been spending more and more time together.'

'Oh,' Neil threw back his head, 'I wish I 'adn't said anything. I wouldn't 'ave if I thought you were going to crack up over it. Just forget it ok, chill out.'

Neil surreptitiously looked at his watch, whilst Desmond continued talking.

'I asked Hannah about it, when I saw her in the Futures, the other night. I like her, she's a nice down to earth girl, someone with a bit of integrity. "Good Lord," she said, "Amanda and Tiggy! You're worrying unnecessarily, her and Tiggy have been friends for years. Besides, who would prefer Tiggy over you?" Yeah, come on let's get some lunch, I love their barbecue chicken. Now, Sarge's, the delicatessen near me. Now you're talking, their jerk chicken rolls are to die for.'

Their conversation become less serious, and soon they were joking light-heartedly with each other. They were approaching the nail salon, which was on the other side of the road. Desmond automatically looked across, and saw Nigel waiting outside. He went cold, and his gaze froze on Nigel, as Amanda left the salon. She and Nigel embraced lightly, before walking up the street.

Neil glanced at Desmond, whose expression was rigid, fixed on the backs of Amanda and Nigel, who were walking buoyantly, side by side, talking and laughing with each other. A slight smile played across Neil's lips, and he continued his jovial chatter, but there was no response from Desmond, who looked as if he had been anaesthetised.

Chapter 18

There was an uncomfortable silence, when Amanda entered the house after finishing work that Thursday. She immediately felt apprehensive, it took her back to her school days, as it was the kind of silence that fell over the school when pupils were summoned to the Assembly Hall. There was that air of menace, as they were only called to the Hall to hear bad news. She opened the door to the lounge hesitatingly, to be met with her mother sitting in the armchair by the side of the gas fire, who just stared at her. What is my mother doing sitting there she thought, with a sense of unease? She is normally in the kitchen at this time, busily preparing tea. Why isn't the television on? She looked around for her father, who was just sitting, staring at the wall. Wayne who was sitting on the sofa, had the expression of someone at a funeral, did not turn to look at her. Neil was pacing about the room, he was keyed up, like a shaken bottle of soda. A cold panic gripped Amanda.

'What's 'appened?' she said with alarm.

'Come on, we're going down the 'ospital,' Neil said abruptly.

'Ospital! Why, what, who's in the 'ospital?' Alarm had now turned to fear.

'It's Nigel,' Neil seemed barely able to contain his anger. 'He's been beaten up.'

'B… B… Beaten up!' Amanda stammered in disbelief, and clutched the back of the sofa with one hand. She looked at Mair, who turned her gaze away, then Wayne, then Gerald who did not avert their stares.

'YES, BEATEN UP,' Neil glared at her, his face red, and his nostrils were flared. 'Now get changed, we're going down the 'ospital.'

Amanda ascended the staircase in a daze, a feeling of numbness had taken over her, a feeling of unreality, as if any second now, her mother would go into the kitchen, there would be the clang of pots and pans, the television would be on, and there would be the sound of male voices. She unbuttoned her blouse, her movements were mechanical, as if acting on instinct, rather than having any control. She slipped on a sweatshirt, which she pulled down over her hips. She didn't bother to change out of the skirt she had worn that day at work. Her mind could not seem to accept the situation. Even when the voices started downstairs, she could not register what was being said. Her mother and Neil were shouting at each other. She made her way back downstairs in a stupor. Neil was still striding around the room.

'Come on,' Neil said irritably, his movements were jerky.

She followed him to the car, and was just about to get in, when she heard her mother shouting, and turned to see her running out of the house.

'Wait, you 'aven't 'ad anything to eat yet.'

'I'm not 'ungry,' Amanda mumbled.

'We'll 'ave something when we get back, or call at the chippy,' Neil shouted from the opened door of the car.

Neil's eyes were wide, and his teeth bared, as he forced the car gear forward, and surged out of the street. He drove faster than he normally drove, and he was talking incessantly. Amanda however, was impervious to what he was saying.

'I should 'ave known something like this would 'appen.'

'Ow would you 'ave known?' Amanda muttered.

'That double crossing ape. All I've done for 'im. Being there for 'im. Holding his rotten black hand, through everything. WHAT THE?!' he slammed on the brakes. Amanda lurched forwards, only to be snapped back, by the tautness of the seatbelt. Neil frantically wound down the window.

'YOU BLOODY IDIOT,' he shouted at a youth in his late teens, who stood gaping in front of the car.

'What are you doing?' Neil flicked his hand past his ear. 'Get off the road.'

The youth sauntered to the side of the road, still staring at Neil, he pointed to his temple, with his right finger, which he twisted back and forth.

'Yeah, same to you an all,' Neil shouted, and did the same with his finger.

'Where do you think you are. The Grand Prix?' the youth said scathingly.

'Yeah, I'll see you later pal, then it will be the WBO. What an idiot,' Neil pushed the car back into gear. 'Did you see that?' he said incredulously. 'Lenny was right,' he went back to his rant. 'You can't trust them. Our family showed 'im nothing but 'ospitality, and all the while, he's trying to screw my sister. He screwed us over all right,' Neil hit the steering wheel with both closed fists, when he stopped at traffic lights.

'Wait a minute,' Amanda suddenly came to life, 'surely you don't think Desmond 'ad anything to do with this!

'Who else would it be?' Neil raved, his foot pressed back on the accelerator, body angled against the steering wheel. 'Who else would do something like this? To Nige. Nigel didn't deserve this. There's nothing to 'im. More meat on Lester Piggott's whip. BLACK! He'll be black and blue, when me and Smithy get old of 'im.'

'Desmond wouldn't do something like this!' Amanda said with disbelief.

'Oh, wouldn't he,' Neil said sharply, 'ow well do you know your precious Desmond then? What is it, four, five months? And you think you know 'im inside out.'

'Ow can you be so sure Desmond did this. Where's your evidence?' Amanda demanded.

'Oh, I know alright. And a tall, black man was seen standing not far from the gully where Nigel was found.'

'Who said that? 'Ow can you believe them? Even if there was a man seen near the area, it doesn't mean it was the man who beat Nigel up. And not every black man is Desmond.'

'Ow many black men 'ave you seen walking about Aedre, ay?'

Amanda exhaled long and loudly.

'I should 'ave known, I should 'ave known,' Neil continued, the words rushing out of his mouth. 'I rue the day I met 'im, and certainly wish I 'ad never invited 'im to the 'ouse.'

'You believe the people who said they saw a black man in the area?'

'OH, I believe them alright. That black son of a bitch.'

'Wait, before jumping to conclusions, let's see what Nigel 'as to say.'

'He's covering for the son of a bitch in 'e. Said he didn't see who attacked 'im. That's the type of boy Nigel is. Doesn't want to get 'im into trouble, even after what that black piece of rubbish did. He doesn't deserve this kind of consideration. If only he had the ounce of decency Nigel 'as. I reckon Nigel is thinking of you,' Neil shot Amanda a glance, who became alert at seeing the hospital in front of her. 'Nigel knows how upset you will be, realising Desmond did something like this, and he doesn't want to upset you.'

Amanda clambered out of the car, as soon as it came to a halt. She raced across the car park, pushed through the thick, glass, double doors to the acrid smell of disinfectant, which burnt her nostrils.

'Can you tell me which ward Nigel Barker is in please?' she managed to ask the receptionist, through frantic breaths, both her palms were on the counter.

'Room C3 love.'

Amanda was halfway up the corridor, and through a set of swing doors, before the receptionist had ended her sentence, in which she was giving directions. She practically sprinted along the tortuous corridor, ran up the stairs, taking three at a time, quickly followed by Neil, until she reached Nigel's room. Her body went rigid at the sight of Nigel. His mother, father and sister were sitting at his bedside. They all looked at Amanda, who stood staring fixedly from the doorway. His mother had a shattered look.

'Oh Nigel, what's 'appened to you?' Amanda's voice was choked with emotion, as she tentatively walked towards him. The sting of salt was in her eyes and on her cheeks, as tears ran down her face.

She flung herself on the bed, careful not to put too much pressure on Nigel. Nigel was sitting up in bed, but his face was coloured black, grey and purple, to the extent, he was hardly recognisable. She could hear Neil's voice through her sobs, as he spoke to Nigel's family, and her ear distinguished the individual voices.

'I didn't recognise 'im,' she heard Nigel's mother say.

'Ave the police got any further?' Neil asked.

Amanda did not know how long she had lain prostrate across the bed, before she felt Neil gently pulling at her shoulders. 'It's time to go now,' he said softly.

'Nigel,' she said gently from a sitting position, her throat straining with sadness, 'please, answer me truthfully.' There was a long pause, 'Did Desmond do this to you?' she struggled to ask.

He looked towards Neil who was standing in the doorway, whilst Amanda waited expectantly.

He kept his eyes on Neil the whole time. 'I didn't see anyone, it was too dark,' he mumbled through swollen lips, still looking directly at Neil.

'That must ave been difficult, beating up a kid like Nigel,' Lenny was strutting before Desmond and the men working at their machines, the following Monday at work. There seemed to be a glow on his face. 'Well, I 'ope it was worth it, cause you ain't got any friends yere now.'

'Yeah, you were out of order,' came a voice from the crowd of workers.

'I mean Nigel didn't deserve that,' Smithy said derisively. 'I mean, 'e's only a whippersnapper.'

'What's the point of me disagreeing with you?' Desmond said rhetorically. 'Seems to me, you've all decided I'm guilty.'

'Why would you be around Duke Street at nine o'clock on a Wednesday night?' Lenny lifted his shoulders and flat palms to the ceiling, his chest puffed out. 'Looking to buy some mangos were you?'

'I wasn't here on Wednesday night, and there is more than one witness who can vouch for that.'

'Oh yeah, and they're all Sambos are they?'

'I didn't do it, OK?' Desmond's voice was raised.

'So why would someone yere say you were yere then. Are you trying to say Aedre people are liars?' Lenny stood before him, with raised eyebrows.

'Looks like someone is trying to set me up,' Desmond lowered his voice back down.

'Huh,' Lenny exclaimed, and walked back to his work bench. 'Who would beat up a skinny kid, just to get at you? What type of people do you think we are yere? We are not like you. We do not lie and steal.'

'Steady on now Lenny,' Smithy came forward from behind his bench.

'Are you calling me a thief?' Desmond's voice was raised again, eyes glaring.

'Calm down Desmond,' Smithy raised both palms pacifyingly towards him. 'Feelings are running high in the community over what's 'appened.'

'The lad said he did not see who had done it,' Desmond said adamantly.

'Did you threaten 'im?' Lenny said cockily. 'Is that why 'e won't talk?'

'Lenny, THAT'S ENOUGH,' said Smithy, 'now get back to your bench.'

'Are you siding with 'im now?'

'I'm not siding with anyone. I think we should let the police sort this out.'

'I DID NOT BEAT THAT BOY. You're very sure of yourself,' Desmond walked up to Lenny, and prodded him on the shoulder. 'Well, let's step outside, and see just how much of a man you are.'

The other men left their benches and stood behind Lenny.

'You mean,' Lenny said with self-assurance, 'you'll give me a good beating, because you are twice the size of me. Well, you're going to 'ave to take us all on.'

'You're brave when you have backing. I wonder if you'll have the same courage if I run into you alone. If any of you want to face me in a fair fight, I will do so. But all of my family have sweated blood and tears for this country. We have never claimed anything from the state. The next person who calls me, or any of my family a liar and a thief, I will kill.'

'Ok, let's cool things now, and get back to work,' said Smithy, as he placed his hand on Lenny's back, and guided him back to his bench. 'This thing has caused enough hatred as it is. We don't want a riot, there has been enough grief already, we don't want any more beatings.'

All the men went sheepishly back to their benches.

'Oh, don't you start on me now,' Desmond threw up his hands in despair, whilst talking to Amanda outside the factory at lunchtime. 'I've had enough from that lot this morning,' he jerked his thumb towards the factory. 'Why don't you believe me?'

'I don't know what to believe any more,' Amanda said sadly.

After returning from the hospital that night, Amanda had spent about forty minutes studying her face in the mirror, after she had slowly taken off all her makeup. Her skin looked bone white. She had also noticed the pink lines, left by the elastic of her tights, across her soft stomach.

'Is that what you think of me? That I could beat a boy like that? A boy whose nose I could probably break, with the flick of my finger?'

'You've changed Desmond, and I don't know why. In the beginning, it was so wonderful. Then you looked at me, as if you couldn't bear to be without me. Now, you look at me as if you hate me. We can't 'ave a decent conversation any longer. Every time we try to talk, we end up arguing.'

'Yeah, well you've changed as well,' he said sullenly.

'I 'aven't changed,' Amanda said stubbornly.

'Maybe then, you aren't the person I thought you were.'

'I am who I am. I don't pretend to be anybody else.' His words prickled hot, under her skin. 'Lately, I've only 'ad to mention Nigel and you go off on one. So what am I supposed to believe?'

'Ok, you can ask me this once. This once, we'll get it out of the way, and then I don't want to hear it ever again.'

Amanda looked directly into Desmond's eyes.

'Tell me the truth. Did you beat up Nigel?'

Desmond looked directly back at her.

'No.'

Chapter 19

'I loved you too much,' Desmond snapped loudly, his body shaking, eyes staring straight ahead, hands tightly gripped to the steering wheel. He was driving over the Sceard, and darkness clung around them. Budweiser was boiling in his blood, and his breath smelt of concentrated alcohol. 'When I first met you, it was as if I had been transported to another world. My life changed in a way I could never have imagined. I then realised what life was all about. The meaning I had been searching for.' Words were just tumbling out of his mouth, and it scared Amanda. There was a fury behind his eyes. 'That mind numbing job. Going down the Bewhearf every weekend. Getting up, going to work. Then you came into my life, and suddenly, everything was good.' He felt tears burning his eyes. The emotion in his voice, which he had suppressed for days, now came pouring out. 'I didn't mind going to work each morning. Driving between these beautiful mountains, because at least I would be within a mile of you. I couldn't wait to be with you. I would be looking at the clock, waiting for it to hit four, so I could rush to be with you sooner, or hear your voice on the phone. Now, I wish I'd never met you,' his shout was like the crack of the starting pistol, which she heard on sports day at school.

There was a fierceness to him, that she had never seen before. As if a lightning storm, was brewing up inside him. His eyes were no longer soft and brown, but dark and cruel. Bitter, with brewed emotions. The flesh was sunken, underneath his eyes.

'Oh don't say that. 'Ow can you say that?' Amanda said pleadingly. 'All I've ever done is love you. From the moment

I saw you, all I've ever wanted is you.' She looked out of the window, but could see nothing, apart from what was directly in the glow of the headlights, which lit up the row of cat's eyes, glaring with menace from the tarmac. The marks of where his fingers had dug into the flesh of her upper arm earlier, were still visible. She pulled down the sleeves of her blouse to cover them, as if covering a tattoo. He had slammed the car door, after she had got in, with punishing force.

'What a fool I've been,' Desmond was shaking his head, but his focus was straight ahead. 'You showed me paradise, and I was fool enough to believe it.' There was a distracted brittle edge to his voice. The pain he had felt, on seeing Amanda and Nigel together, was as intense as if his hand had been caught in the cutting machine he worked on. He could not get rid of the image of them together. Since then, it was as if he had picked up a virus, which was destroying him. They may have been lost in a crowd, but he could not lose them. Even at night, when he closed his eyes, he could still see them, imprinted on his retina. The broad smiles as they looked at one another, oblivious to their surroundings. The wound had got under his skin, and it would never heal. The neon signs in the shop windows, every time he passed, seemed to be saying fool. 'I should have listened to people, but I was blinded. They tried to tell me.'

'Why do you listen to people?' Amanda's voice dissolved with tears, 'it's just not true. Why don't you believe me?'

'YOUR OWN BROTHER,' Desmond yelled. 'Why would your brother lie to me?'

'I can't believe Neil is doing this to me. He doesn't want us to be together. I don't care what he wants. All I want is you, and I'm prepared to give up everything for you.' She looked at Desmond, but was met with an unbelieving stare. She realised it didn't matter what she said, he would not believe her. 'Well screw you Des, if you can't see how much I love you.'

'Well that's just great Amanda. Did you take debating lessons to argue like that? It's not what I've been *told* you see,' he emphasised the word told. 'It's what I've seen.'

Amanda turned again to look at him, her mouth was open, and eyes wide, she wanted to say something, but was speechless.

'I was walking through the high street last Tuesday at lunch time. And of course, I could not walk past the salon, without looking over to see if I could catch a glimpse of you. Oh, I caught a glimpse alright. There you were, meeting lover boy. Walking arm and arm down the street, with your precious *Tiggy*, with eyes only for each other, as if you were the only two people in the world.'

'Oh God Desmond, we're just friends. How many times 'ave I told you that? It would be impossible for me to see Nigel any other way. We are like brother and sister,' she spluttered.

'You could have fooled me,' his words were weighted with contempt. Rage surged through his body, like a current of electricity. 'You care nothing for me. My father was right,' he spat the words out, as if they tasted bitter. 'White women are no good. They don't look after you, and they go with other men.' He was driving straight on a meandering road, no attempt at negotiating curves. On grass, then back onto road, as if transferring his rage to the accelerator.

'Desmond, what are you doing?' Amanda was white and rigid, gripping the sides of her seat.

'Of course, I didn't listen to him. We never do. If I had a son, I would warn him, but, as soon as they see that vision of womanhood before them, all words of wisdom will fly out of the window.'

'YOU 'AVE TO BELIVE ME,' Amanda shrieked. 'There has never been anything between me and Nigel,' she remained rigid, staring straight ahead, still gripping the sides of the chair, her knuckles were white.

'You care nothing for me,' Desmond wound down the window, tore the pink crystal pendant he had bought her, from around her neck, and threw it out of the window with childish spite.

'Oh please Desmond,' Amanda begged. She was cold with terror.

'How could I have not seen?' A line of tears trickled down his cheek, as he continued his dialogue.

'Desmond slow down,' Amanda said with fear, her heart was slamming against her chest.

The landscape suddenly changed, spinning and lurching. A large, tree loomed before them.

'DESMOND STOP!' Amanda screamed.

Epilogue

'So, that was our last date.'

'That's quite a story,' Darren conceded, 'how do you feel now?'

'I'm ok.'

'Good, so are you ready to go home now?'

'No, drive around a bit longer. I don't want my mother to see me in this state.'

'You seem a lot calmer now, although, you are still very pale. Do you ever see Desmond?'

'Every day, even though he doesn't see me.'

'Is he with someone else?'

'He's been with Katrina for two months now. He's known her for about six months. She has been 'elping 'im get over me.'

'And are you over him. Are you seeing anybody?'

'Oh no, me and Desmond will be together one day. A love like ours doesn't die. I'm waiting for 'im.'

'And you could be waiting forever.'

'If that's what it takes.'

'That's not healthy, I think you need to move on. It sounds as if he has. 'When me and Desmond got together, a force was created. That force cannot be destroyed,' Amanda glared at Darren.

'You have been apart for a year,' Darren said emphatically, 'and he has met someone else. I think you need to stop seeing him every day. You need to stop living in this lover's past. It's a form of obsession.'

'She can't take my place. She doesn't realise it, and neither does Desmond,' Amanda said defiantly.

'Is she the same colour as him?'

'Yes.'

'Does he still keep in touch with Neil.'

'Oh no, he was devastated when he realised 'ow Neil had betrayed 'im.'

'He realises then, there was never anything between you and Nigel?'

'Deep down he does.'

'And yet he didn't go back to you. I think you are deluded, by thinking he will. If that was the case, he would have done so before now. Yet you think things will be the same someday.'

'Oh no, not the same, it will be better.'

'But he's with somebody else,' Darren said a little exasperatedly.

'Too much 'appened. It will take a long time to right itself, but it will eventually.'

Darren shook his head.

'Maybe he realises the problems that were caused by his colour, and he's found someone who will be accepted into his family, and likewise, he will be accepted into hers.'

'There will be no prejudices when we get back together.'

'In an ideal world. I wish I could believe that. I think we will progress as a society, but racial tolerance is years into the future, and even then, I think it will still exist on some level. There is hope though, I asked my little niece the other day, if she was still friends with that nice little Chinese girl. She looked at me as if I was mad. "She's Welsh," she said.'

'There is a world of love and harmony.'

'I think you may have hit your head in the accident,' he said mockingly. 'Look, you're talking about getting back with Desmond, as if it is fact. You're wasting your time. You've got your whole life ahead of you. You should be enjoying yourself. From what I can gather, Desmond does not feel the same way you do.'

'Nothing can divide me and Desmond,' Amanda said hotly.

'Ok, ok,' Darren lifted his hands momentarily in resignation. 'So who were you with tonight then. Was it Nigel, who was in the car with you?'

'Oh no, he's with Rosaline, and I'm so 'appy for them.'

'So what happened with her and Neil?'

'Once she realised what kind of person Neil was, that was it.' Darren started to say something, but became distracted by a street sign, 'Isn't this your street?'

'Yeah, that's my 'ouse over there, on the left. The one with the green door.'

Darren pulled his car to the edge of the kerb, came to a halt, turned the key in the ignition, and the engine took its last breath.

'Are you alright?' he looked at Amanda with concern.

'Yeah, I'm alright,' Amanda nodded

'You stay there, and I'll go get someone.' Darren glanced at his watch, as he got out of the car. He hoped his wife was asleep, as it was at least another twenty-minute drive to his home. He looked up the street, there were no lights behind the windows of the houses. The street was asleep, nothing was stirring. There was a stiffness in his legs, which made the walk up the garden steps a bit of an obstacle. It occurred to Darren how late it was, and the difficulty of the news he had to deliver. He looked for signs of life in the house, but there was not a flicker of light or murmur of sound. He found that strange, due to the hour. He would have thought someone would be waiting for their daughter. Times had changed however, since he was a youth. He was apprehensive about knocking the door, and stood outside for a few minutes, trying to form the words he would say to the house occupant. He took a deep breath, and knocked with just enough force to wake someone in the household, as opposed to anyone else in the street.

After a short time, he heard the sound of something moving, way behind the door. Then came the sound of padded slippers, shuffling across a floor. Darren felt a rush of blood around his body. He scraped a hand through his hair.

The door was opened by a woman who looked to be in her late fifties, or early sixties, but Darren had the feeling she was younger than she looked. She wore a faded pink dressing gown, and had a worn, grey look. Darren cleared his throat.

'Mrs Williams,' he said a little awkwardly.

'Yes,' the woman said with slight annoyance, yet curiosity.

'Amanda is sitting in the car, just down there. I'm afraid she's been in an accident, and is a little shaken up.'

The woman just stared at him.

'I, I know this must be quite a shock,' he stammered.

Still the woman just stared at him. Darren shuffled around on his feet, wondering what he should do next. Should he go and get Amanda?

'Is this some kind of sick joke?' the woman at last spoke.

Darren looked at her in astonishment, lost for words.

'No, no,' he extended an arm, open palmed, fingers spread towards the car. He looked at the car, then back at the woman frantically.

'My daughter was killed in a car crash a year ago,' the woman said coldly, before turning back into the house, and slamming the door.

Darren stood staring at the door for a few seconds, before rushing to the car. Amanda was not in the car. He looked wildly around, and down the street. There was no sign of her. He ran over to the passenger side, and yanked open the car door. He searched the seat and floor for signs of blood. There was nothing, not a trace. There was however, the faint tang of her perfume. He felt the seat, but it was stone cold. He stood upright, and scanned the street again. The only sound was of a can being tossed across the street, by the wind. The sound echoed down the street, until the bouncing can came to a rest at the kerb. The street which was bathed in orange light, was uncannily still. The wind whistled eerily through the telephone wires.

The White Lady of the Bwlch

There is a myth in the Rhondda, that late one evening, a lone driver, driving over the Bwlch mountain road, comes across a young woman of approximately twenty to twenty- five years of age, hitch-hiking.

Not wanting her to come to any harm, he stops and offers her a lift. She gets into the car and gives directions. On reaching her house, she asks if he can get her mother. He agrees, and knocks on the door, which is answered by an elderly lady. He explains her daughter is in the car, to which the woman replies, there must be a mistake, as her daughter had died in a car accident some years ago.

He returns shaken to the car, to find there is no trace of anyone in or near the car.

Acknowlegements

Mei Lin Ng for her continued friendship, support and advice.

My cousin Kim Rydelewski for persuading me to write another novel.

My mother.

My father John Barnes
26 October 1934 – 8 November 2020
Missed by many.

My husband William for his support. It cannot be easy being married to a writer.

Mahmood Mattan 1922 – 1952, for the injustice he suffered, just for falling in love with a woman of a different colour skin.

#BlackLivesMatter

The Windrush Generation, and citizens from other countries who came to make Britain a better place.